Samuel French Acting Edition

Popcorn Falls

by James Hindman

SAMUELFRENCH.COM   SAMUELFRENCH.CO.UK

FOR PRODUCTION ENQUIRIES

UNITED STATES AND CANADA
Info@SamuelFrench.com
1-866-598-8449

UNITED KINGDOM AND EUROPE
Abrams Artists Agency
275 Seventh Avenue, 26th floor
New York, NY 10001
Attention: Charles Kopelman
charles.kopelman@abramsartistsagency.com
646-486-4600

Each title is subject to availability from Samuel French, depending
upon country of performance. Please be aware that *POPCORN FALLS*
may not be licensed by Samuel French in your territory. Professional
and amateur producers should contact the nearest Samuel French
office or licensing partner to verify availability.

MUSIC USE NOTE

Licensees are solely responsible for obtaining formal written permission from copyright owners to use copyrighted music in the performance of this play and are strongly cautioned to do so. If no such permission is obtained by the licensee, then the licensee must use only original music that the licensee owns and controls. Licensees are solely responsible and liable for all music clearances and shall indemnify the copyright owners of the play(s) and their licensing agent, Samuel French, against any costs, expenses, losses and liabilities arising from the use of music by licensees. Please contact the appropriate music licensing authority in your territory for the rights to any incidental music.

IMPORTANT BILLING AND CREDIT REQUIREMENTS

If you have obtained performance rights to this title, please refer to your licensing agreement for important billing and credit requirements.

POPCORN FALLS had its world premiere at Theatre NOVA (Carla Milarch, Founding Artistic Director; Diane Hill, Producing Artistic Director) on January 20, 2017. The production was directed by Daniel C. Walker, with original sound design by Carla Milarch, and set and lighting design by Daneil C. Walker. The stage manager was Emily-Ann Jugowicz. The cast was as follows:

ACTOR 1 . . . . Jeff Priskorn

ACTOR 2 . . . . .Jonathan Jones

POPCORN FALLS was produced and developed at the Riverbank Theatre (Kathy Vertin, Artistic Director) from May 24–27, 2018. The production was directed by Christian Borle, with original music and sound design by Jeffrey Lodin, costume design by Joseph La Corte, and set design by Tom Vertin. The cast was as follows:

ACTOR 1 . . . . .James Hindman

ACTOR 2 . . . . Tom Souhrada

POPCORN FALLS premiered Off Broadway at the Davenport Theatre in New York City on October 8, 2018 (produced by Schondeikkan Productions and D.T.R. Productions). The production was directed by Christian Borle, with original music and sound design by Jeffrey Lodin, set design by Tim Mackabee, costume design by Joseph La Corte, and lighting design by Jeff Croiter. The general manager was Cheryl Dennis and the production stage manager was Yetti Steinman. The cast was as follows:

ACTOR 1 . . . . Adam Heller

ACTOR 2 . . . . Tom Souhrada

CHARACTERS

MR. TRUNDLE (1) – A sincere man. People-pleaser. The new mayor of Popcorn Falls. Recently divorced and a recovered alcoholic, determined to pull his life back together.

JOE (2) – A nervous janitor whose wife is pregnant with their third set of twins.

PASTOR PETE – With donations at an all-time low, his church has no money to fix its drooping steeple. Uses a walker to get around.

MRS. OMKI – With the building of a local Walmart, she now has nowhere to park her Tart Cart. Speaks with a very flat Midwest accent.

AUSTIN – The not-very-bright-but-eager-to-please sheriff of Popcorn Falls. Would like everyone to think he's smarter and more important than he actually is. Wants desperately to make his mother proud and become the next chief of police. Could speak with a bit of a southern accent.

MS. LYDA PARKER – Town librarian. A bit Amanda Wingfield from *The Glass Menagerie*. A theatrical woman of a certain age. Was once the leading lady of the Anchor Bay Players. Speaks with a Mid-Atlantic accent. Always carrying her cat, Mr. Cuddles.

FLOYD – Owner of the only lumberyard in town. Lost half his arm in a freak accident involving a telephone pole and a Mexican stripper. Likes to drink...a lot. Was once in love with Mrs. Stepp.

MRS. STEPP – Hard-boiled, chain-smoking, no-nonsense middle school teacher who is on the prowl. Secretly still has a thing for Floyd. Always looks like she's holding a cigarette.

MR. DOYLE – Head of the Cattaraugus County Budget Planning Committee. Determined. A corrupt bully who will stop at nothing to conquer Popcorn Falls and turn it into a sewage treatment plant.

MISS BROWN – Mr. Doyle's very unenthusiastic secretary. Would rather be doing anything else.

BECKY A very sweet, lost soul. Just moved back to Popcorn Falls. Was once in love with Joe.

HANS – Originally from Germany, Hans came to Popcorn Falls as a foreign exchange student and stayed. He now runs the Popcorn Falls Funeral Home and is obsessed with Fred Astaire and Ginger Rogers movies. He speaks with a heavy German accent, wears a monocle, and is very excited to be part of the new acting troupe.

MARGIE – A high school senior who is obsessed with herself and her phone. She speaks with a flat, drawn-out, monotone voice.

MR. UPMALL – The oldest man in Popcorn Falls. Wants to do something great before he dies. Walks with a cane and a slow shuffle.

LYDIA – Becky's young daughter.

AUTHOR'S NOTE

Two actors play the entire population of Popcorn Falls. The numbers next to each character's name (1 and 2) indicate which actor plays which role. There are minimal set pieces and virtually no costumes. We will know the character by the actor's physicality and the addition of a hat or pair of glasses. The simpler, the better. For example, a sweater can become a cat; an actor can take a shirt, wrap it around his waist, and it becomes an apron.

MUSIC NOTE

Music can play as the actors write on the chalkboard and transition from one scene to the next. There are music cues throughout the script that indicate where music was used to cover the scene changes. This music is optional. Performance tracks with original music by Jeffrey Lodin are available for licensing through Samuel French.

ACKNOWLEDGEMENTS

The playwright would like to thank Tom Souhrada, Christian Borle, Jeffrey Lodin, Joseph La Corte, Lynne Halliday, Joanna Allen Lodin, Charles Kopelman, Eric Sweeney, Jonathan and Irit Kolber, Robert and Natalie Hindman, Brian and Renee Fonville, Mark and Ginny Zeffiro, Lesley Stewart Grilley, Tom and Kathy Vertin, Austin Murphy, Daniel C. Walker, Arlene Hutton, The Barrow Group, and The Protagonists Union.

To John and our parents,
Gerald and Virginia Hindman, John and Shirley Ploetz

"The citizens of America are, from this period, to be considered as the actors on a most conspicuous theatre, which seems to be peculiarly designated by Providence for the display of human greatness and felicity."

– George Washington

Scene One: Town Hall

(We are on the stage of the town hall in the small town of Popcorn Falls. An American flag stands in one corner next to a small bookcase, two chairs, and a small table. A chalkboard sits upstage center with a crude drawing of a huge water spigot gushing water. A microphone is set off to one side. A sign overhead reads "Welcome to Popcorn Falls.")

[MUSIC NO. 01]

VOICE-OVER. Hello, and welcome to the historic town hall, nestled quaintly in the heart of picturesque Popcorn Falls. Please take a moment to turn off all cellular devices, and keep all arms, legs and handbags out of the aisle. Now enjoy your stay in Popcorn Falls.

(Before the announcement finishes, the lights flicker and the music and voice warp as if the power has gone out. The stage goes black for one second, then in the dark a melodramatic piece of opera music is played:)

[MUSIC NO. 02]

(The lights bump up, now dark and mysterious. Two men enter from either side of the stage looking scared to death. They meet center and look out to the audience... "Oh no!" When the music kicks into high gear, the men run around setting up for the top of the show and erase the board. **JOE** *hurries to the back of the house as* **MR. TRUNDLE** *grabs the mic stand and sets it downstage center. As the*

stand hits the ground, the music ends and the lights come up full. **MR. TRUNDLE** *speaks into the mic as if nothing just happened.)*

MR. TRUNDLE 1. *(Rehearsing in a calm, flat tone.)* Good evening, ladies and gentlemen. As the new mayor of Popcorn Falls, it gives me great pleasure to introduce the chief executive officer of Cattaraugus County, Mr. Doyle. He brings wonderful news about our future. How about a big Popcorn...how about a big...how about a big...

(Tapping on the mic.) Hello? Hello? Joe? Can you hear me? Testing one, two...testing...

(Shouts to the back of the room.) Joe? Hey, Joe?!

JOE 2. *(Offstage.)* What do you need, Mr. Trundle?!

MR. TRUNDLE 1. *(Loudly.)* Can you hear me?!

JOE 2. *(Offstage.)* Yeah!

MR. TRUNDLE 1. *(Yelling offstage.)* No, I mean can you hear me through the...

(Quietly into mic.) Sibilance, sibilance...

(Yelling offstage.) Can you hear me now?!

JOE 2. *(Offstage.)* Loud and clear! Can you hear me?!

MR. TRUNDLE 1. Well, sure I can, but...

JOE 2. *(Offstage.)* Try talking into the mic!

MR. TRUNDLE 1. I just did.

JOE 2. *(Offstage.)* When?

MR. TRUNDLE 1. Just now!

JOE 2. *(Offstage.)* I can hear ya fine!

MR. TRUNDLE 1. I don't mean *now*, I mean...!

(Quietly into mic.) Bubble gum, bubble gum, bubble gum.

(Yelling again.) Joe, what's the point of having a mic if I have to yell?!

*(**JOE** enters.)*

JOE 2. You don't have to yell. Just step up and talk directly into the... *(Spotting the mic cord.)* No.

MR. TRUNDLE 1. What?

JOE 2. No!

MR. TRUNDLE 1. Joe, what's the matter?

>   (**JOE** *picks up the frayed end of the mic cord.*)

JOE 2. It's that squirrel!

MR. TRUNDLE 1. What squirrel?

JOE 2. That squirrel! I told the county this would happen! *(Looking around.)* Where are you?!

MR. TRUNDLE 1. Joe, since when do we have squirrels in the town hall?

JOE 2. Since we can't afford squirrel traps. The county won't give us money to buy anything!
(Exiting.) I know you're here somewhere!

>   (*He runs off, looking for the squirrel.* **MR. TRUNDLE** *yells after him:*)

MR. TRUNDLE 1. Joe, we need to find a microphone. This room is about to be filled with people! With a lot of very angry people!

>   (**JOE** *enters as* **PASTOR PETE**, *wearing glasses and an ill-fitting clerical collar. He mimes using a walker.*)

PASTOR PETE 2. Can we come in yet?

MR. TRUNDLE 1. Five more minutes, Father!

PASTOR PETE 2. But my steeple is drooping! This has never happened to me before.

MR. TRUNDLE 1. *(Ushering him out.)* We're gonna get your steeple standing at attention, Father!
(Yelling offstage.) Thank you in advance for your forgiveness!

JOE 2. *(Offstage.)* Come out, come out, wherever you are, Mr. Squirrel!

MR. TRUNDLE 1. *(Yelling offstage.)* Joe, what are we going to do? The people have to hear Doyle! They need to hear about the check!

(**JOE** *enters on the other side of the stage as* **MRS. OMKI**. *His rag is folded over her head and held under her chin like a babushka. She speaks with a very flat accent.*)

MRS. OMKI 2. When is this meeting going to start?

MR. TRUNDLE 1. Four more minutes!

MRS. OMKI 2. They put up a Walmart right where I used to park my Tart Cart! I mean, what the fart?!

MR. TRUNDLE 1. *(Ushering her out.)* I will issue you a new vender's permit, Mrs. Omki!
(Yelling offstage.) We're gonna let you park that Tart Cart right in the heart of Artberry Park! Dream big!

JOE 2. *(Entering.)* This is what happens when a town goes bankrupt, Mr. Trundle. This is what happens when the town next to you builds a dam that ruins your waterfall.

(*He taps on the mic.*)

And this is what happens when your waterfall dries up and you haven't seen a tourist in three years!

(*He flips the switch on the wall sconce; it doesn't work. The Popcorn Falls sign falls to one side with a thud.*)

MR. TRUNDLE 1. You know what, I kind of like it. *[If there is no sign: "Dear, God, not even a light bulb?"]*

JOE 2. Nothing in this town works anymore. And we're the next to go.

(*He heads offstage.*)

MR. TRUNDLE 1. They're not going to fire us, Joe.
(Yelling offstage.) I'm the mayor! They can't fire the mayor! And you, you're the...head custodian.

JOE 2. *(Offstage.)* Executive Custodian!

MR. TRUNDLE 1. Executive Custodian! This town would fall apart if it weren't for you!

(**JOE** *enters from the opposite side of the stage as* **MS. LYDA PARKER**, *an elderly theatrical woman with a Mid-Atlantic accent. She* *grabs a sweater from the coat rack, making a loud screech. The sweater becomes her cat, Mr. Cuddles.)*

MS. PARKER 2. *(Grabbing sweater, cat screech.)* Mr. Trundle!

MR. TRUNDLE 1. Ms. Parker.

MS. PARKER 2. Mr. Cuddles and I have been waiting for over three hours!

MR. TRUNDLE 1. Then what's three more minutes?

MS. PARKER 2. Twenty-eight years I have devoted my life to the Popcorn Falls Library...

MS. PARKER 2 & MR. TRUNDLE 1. ...Twenty-nine, this April.

MR. TRUNDLE 1. Yes, I remember. Now, if you wouldn't mind waiting outside.

MS. PARKER 2. That building is a hundred and twenty-three years old. George Washington dined on that very land.

MR. TRUNDLE 1. Well, it was a picnic lunch, Ms. Parker. Perspective.

(Ushering her offstage.) Now, if I could please ask you to wait outside.

(Yelling offstage.) I promise I'll save Mr. Cuddles a seat!

JOE 2. *(Offstage.)* I can't move! I can't move!

MR. TRUNDLE 1. Joe... Joe, what happened?!

(Walking offstage.) Are you okay? Should I call a doctor?

> (**JOE** *enters from the other side carrying a small, mesh trash can and a bag of garbage.* **MR. TRUNDLE** *follows him on.)*

JOE 2. No, I mean, I can't move! I can't sell my house! Who's going to buy a house in a town that's bankrupt?

MR. TRUNDLE 1. *(Grabbing the trash can.)* We are not going bankrupt. Will you listen to me?! Doyle said he has a whole new understanding of the situation and that he will be here tonight with a check.

> (**JOE** *continues offstage with the garbage.* **MR. TRUNDLE** *yells after him:)*

He's going to present us with a huge check, Joe! We have Doyle right where we want him.

(JOE re-enters as FLOYD, the one-armed lumberyard owner. This is accomplished by his holding his hand in his armpit.)

FLOYD 2. Mr. Trundle!

MR. TRUNDLE 1. Two more minutes, Floyd.

FLOYD 2. What am I supposed to do with all that lumber you told me to buy?!

MR. TRUNDLE 1. Floyd, you know very well I never told you to buy anything.

(He places the trash can down.)

FLOYD 2. Six months ago you stood on this stage and promised a housing boom and I was first to raise my hand in support!

MR. TRUNDLE 1. And I appreciate it.

FLOYD 2. You promised progress, Mr. Trundle! Hope! Change!

(MR. TRUNDLE leads FLOYD out the door.)

MR. TRUNDLE 1. Change is at the front door, Floyd. Entering the building as we speak.

(Out front.) Now, if everyone could please, please, please use the front door!

(JOE enters. MR. TRUNDLE puts the small table and chair in place, then goes off to grab a small vase with a single flower.)

JOE 2. And Doyle knew what he was doing when he built that dam. That's a lot of water to reroute. That's a big dam you have to build to hold back a lot of water. And for what?

MR. TRUNDLE 1. Water?

JOE 2. For water. For money. So their town could grow. And what do we have?

MR. TRUNDLE 1. No water?

JOE 2. A dry riverbed and a wall of rocks covered in graffiti, "Welcome to Popcorn Balls!"

(Picking up mic cord.) We've been eaten, Mr. Trundle. They're the squirrel, we're the cord.

MR. TRUNDLE 1. A mic cord! We need a new mic cord, Joe!

> (*He rushes offstage to hunt for a mic cord.* **JOE** *sits, becoming emotional.*)

JOE 2. That was a very important waterfall, Mr. Trundle.

MR. TRUNDLE 1. (*Popping his head onstage.*) I know.

JOE 2. George Washington and his men stopped there. They gained nourishment to win independence for America.

MR. TRUNDLE 1. (*Popping head onstage again.*) I know.

JOE 2. (*Breaking down crying.*) That waterfall is a very important part of the history of the United States.

MR. TRUNDLE 1. (*Entering.*) Oh my god... Oh my god, Trudy's pregnant again.

JOE 2. (*Crying.*) This is about our waterfall!

MR. TRUNDLE 1. Your wife's about to have a baby and you don't know if you're going to have a job in two weeks.

JOE 2. The doctor hears two heartbeats.

MR. TRUNDLE 1. Well that's...

JOE 2. Twins!

MR. TRUNDLE 1. Congratulations!

JOE 2. We have two sets of twins now! What are the odds?!

> (**MR. TRUNDLE** *moves the mic to the side of the stage.*)

MR. TRUNDLE 1. We're all just going to have to talk really loud!

> (**AUSTIN**, *the not-very-bright-but-eager-to-please sheriff of Popcorn, enters, speaking into his walkie-talkie [an eraser from the chalkboard]. His other hand holds his stun gun [another eraser].*)

AUSTIN 2. Three fourteen, three fourteen, this is Sheriff Austin reporting to Mayor Trundle! Mayor Trundle, what's your "twenty"?

> (**MR. TRUNDLE** *approaches* **AUSTIN**.)

MR. TRUNDLE 1. Austin...

(**AUSTIN** *turns to* **MR. TRUNDLE**, *accidentally zapping him with his stun gun.*)

MR. TRUNDLE 1. Ooooow!

AUSTIN 2. *(Turning front.)* Got my stun gun and I am ready for the impending riots.

MR. TRUNDLE 1. Austin...

(**AUSTIN** *turns back to* **MR. TRUNDLE**, *zapping him again.*)

Ooooow!

AUSTIN 2. Got my caution tape, tear gas...

MR. TRUNDLE 1. Austin, look at me *(Claps hands.)* look at me *(Claps hands.)* look at me –

(*Claps hands, points to his own eyes, then to* **AUSTIN**'s.)

Check in! If you want to be helpful, I need you to go outside...

AUSTIN 2. And cool off the crowd with my hose?!

(*He turns to go, but* **MR. TRUNDLE** *grabs his arm and is zapped again.*)

MR. TRUNDLE 1. No... Ooooow! Damn it! Open the doors, Austin! That's all... Just open the doors...!

(**AUSTIN** *heads off.*)

And put down that stun gun before you hurt someone!

(**AUSTIN** *accidentally stuns himself.*)

AUSTIN 2. *(Stun-gun noise.)* Ow!

(**MR. TRUNDLE** *addresses the crowd as they enter.*)

MR. TRUNDLE 1. Okay, everyone, come on in!

(**AUSTIN** *walks down the aisle, ushering the "audience" in like he's backing up a truck.*)

AUSTIN 2. 'Mon back. *[Come on back.]*

MR. TRUNDLE 1. The meeting is about to start!

AUSTIN 2. 'Mon back.

MR. TRUNDLE 1. Plenty of seats up here in the front!

AUSTIN 2. 'Mon back.

MR. TRUNDLE 1. No need to push.

> *(***JOE*** slams down the **AUSTIN** hat and lifts one hand as if holding a cigarette. He is now **MRS. STEPP**, the hard-boiled, no-nonsense, chain-smoking middle school art teacher.)*

MRS. STEPP 2. *(To* **MR. TRUNDLE***.)* You disgust me.

MR. TRUNDLE 1. Not now, Mrs. Stepp.

MRS. STEPP 2. Door to door, I went. Begging people to vote for you. And you have the audacity to cut my budget?

MR. TRUNDLE 1. If everyone could please find a seat.

MRS. STEPP 2. What could possibly be more important than the education of our children?!

> *(***MS. PARKER*** pops out from the other side of **MR. TRUNDLE***.)*

MS. PARKER 2. And those children take books out of my library!

> *(***MR. TRUNDLE*** ushers both ladies up the center aisle.)*

MR. TRUNDLE 1. Ladies, I promise you, all those cuts are about to be reversed.
(To the assembling crowd.) Can you all hear me okay without a mic?

> *(***JOE*** puts the **AUSTIN** hat back on.)*

AUSTIN 2. Mr. Trundle... Mr. Trundle, Mr. Doyle's motorcade just drove up!

> *(***AUSTIN*** goes running up the center aisle.)*

MR. TRUNDLE 1. Thank you, Austin! Show him in! This is it, folks, all our problems are about to be solved.

> *(***JOE*** comes back, wearing thick black glasses. He is now **MR. DOYLE**, shaking the hands of audience members as **MR. TRUNDLE** addresses the crowd.)*

MR. TRUNDLE 1. Good evening, ladies and gentlemen. As the new mayor of Popcorn Falls, it gives me great pleasure to introduce the chief executive officer of Cattaraugus County, Mr. Doyle. He brings wonderful news about our future. How about a big Popcorn shout-out for the man of the hour – Mr. Doyle! *(Applauding.)* Pop! Pop! Pop, pop, pop! Pop! Pop! Pop, pop, pop!

> *(The two men shake hands and pose front. Photo flash.* **MR. DOYLE** *takes the stage while* **MR. TRUNDLE** *steps down to become part of the audience.)*

MR. DOYLE 2. Thank you, Mayor Trundle. Dear citizens of Popcorn.

MR. TRUNDLE 1. Kernels.

MR. DOYLE 2. I beg your pardon?

MR. TRUNDLE 1. *(Referring to audience.)* They like to be addressed as "kernels."

MR. DOYLE 2. *(Through clenched teeth.)* Dear – "Kernels of Popcorn." I have received your budgetary requests and empathize with your predicament...

> *(***MR. TRUNDLE*** *becomes part of the audience by pointing to an audience member as if speaking for them.)*

MR. TRUNDLE 1. *(As audience member.)* We weren't in this predicament until you stole our water! Give us back our falls!

(Hushes audience member.) Don't worry, I've got this!

MR. DOYLE 2. However, we see no other choice but to do the following. In a few short months, boundaries will be redrawn and the town of Popcorn will no longer exist.

MR. TRUNDLE 1. What?!

(Runs up aisle, rousing audience.) Grumble, grumble, rhubarb, rhubarb!

MR. DOYLE 2. And...and! You will be governed by our laws. All town offices...your library, schools, health clinic, community center, city pool, movie theater, post office and the St. Genesius Senior Center...will be closed.

MR. TRUNDLE 1. You can't do that, Mr. Doyle!

(Rousing audience even more!) Bigger grumble! Taller rhubarb!

(As audience member.) Grr!

MR. DOYLE 2. Your downtown area will be demolished and re-purposed into a sewage treatment plant.

MR. TRUNDLE 1. A what?!

MR. DOYLE 2. Providing many needed jobs in your community. Thank you and have a pleasant evening.

MR. TRUNDLE 1. *(Running back onstage.)* Wait! You promised us a check, Mr. Doyle. A huge check.

MR. DOYLE 2. Ah, yes. Some years ago your town requested a grant from the Cattaraugus County Arts Council for the Popcorn Falls Theater. The check is contained in this envelope. I trust you'll get it to the correct administrator.

> *(He hands* **MR. TRUNDLE** *the check, then turns to exit.)*

MR. TRUNDLE 1. Wait. What theater? We don't have a theater.

MR. DOYLE 2. Oh, well, too bad.

> *(Grabs the check from* **MR. TRUNDLE.***)*

I'm sure the Arts Council will find good use for the funds.

MR. TRUNDLE 1. You lied to us, Mr. Doyle.

MR. DOYLE 2. I brought you jobs.

MR. TRUNDLE 1. *(Taking the check from* **MR. DOYLE.***)* A sewage treatment plant?!

MR. DOYLE 2. Job security. Remember, everyone poops.

> *(He gives a quick "two thumbs up." Photo flash.)*

MR. TRUNDLE 1. *(Seeing large amount on check.)* Are you kidding?! This much money could save us! You have to let us keep it!

MR. TRUNDLE 1. *(To audience.)* We could take this money earmarked for the theater that we don't have, and parcel it out to the things we do have. Our library. Our schools.

MR. DOYLE 2. You're welcome to fill out an application.

> *(He grabs the check, but* **MR. TRUNDLE** *doesn't let go. Now they both hold it.)*

MR. TRUNDLE 1. I'll bet that check isn't half as big as the one you'll receive once the sewage treatment plant is built.

MR. DOYLE 2. I beg your pardon?

MR. TRUNDLE 1. I don't suppose your list of investors is public knowledge. How big of a piece do you own?

MR. DOYLE 2. I suggest you think long and hard before you say another word, Mr. Trundle. Long...and hard.

> *(He forcefully pulls the check from* **MR. TRUNDLE** *and exits.* **MR. TRUNDLE** *turns front and addresses the townspeople as they exit.)*

MR. TRUNDLE 1. Before you all leave, I just want to thank everyone for your continued support. And as the new mayor of Popcorn Falls, I'd just like to say...
(Speaking to an empty room, he sits.) ...Shit. Shit!

> *(***JOE*** comes back down the aisle.)*

JOE 2. From the sound of it, there's going to be plenty of that around here.

MR. TRUNDLE 1. I had it!

JOE 2. A theater? He's a liar.

MR. TRUNDLE 1. I had the check in my hand!

JOE 2. No one in this town asked for money to start a theater. We don't need a theater! We need a pothole patcher. We need street lamps.

MR. TRUNDLE 1. *(Idea.)* Wait a minute...

JOE 2. We need squirrel traps!

MR. TRUNDLE 1. Wait a minute. Joe...

JOE 2. Yeah?

MR. TRUNDLE 1. No one took the money for the theater because no one runs a theater.

JOE 2. Uh-huh.

MR. TRUNDLE 1. But if someone ran a theater, they would get the money.

JOE 2. I'm listening.

MR. TRUNDLE 1. And if someone had the money, they could pay off the debt.

JOE 2. Go on.

MR. TRUNDLE 1. And if we paid off the debt we could keep the town open long enough for it to get back on its feet.

JOE 2. Put it together...

MR. TRUNDLE 1. Joe, I know what we're going to do!

JOE 2. What?

MR. TRUNDLE 1. We're gonna put on a play!

JOE 2. We are? What play?

MR. TRUNDLE 1. I don't know. I don't know any plays. *(Looking front.)* Ms. Parker! She's a librarian. She's never been married. She loves cats. She must know about theatre.

> *(Grabs* **JOE** *by the shoulders.)*

Joe, you're a genius.

JOE 2. I am?

> *(***MR. TRUNDLE*** *grabs a gingham shirt from the rack and hands it to* **JOE**.*)*

MR. TRUNDLE 1. Meet me out front in one hour. I gotta swing by the Sudsy Mug. Haven't eaten all day.

JOE 2. Out front in one hour – got it!

MR. TRUNDLE 1. Joe, if we do this...if we pull this off...we are going to save Popcorn Falls!

JOE 2. We are? This is so exciting!

MR. TRUNDLE 1. I know!

[MUSIC NO. 03]

> *(He writes "Sudsy Mug" on the board.)*

Scene Two: Sudsy Mug

(**JOE** *ties the shirt around his waist like an apron and becomes* **BECKY**, *a woman working behind the bar who has the adorable habit of tucking her hair behind her ear. The small bookshelf is turned around to become the counter.* **MR. TRUNDLE** *enters from behind the chalkboard, making a bell sound effect –* "Ding-a-ling.")

BECKY 2. What can I get you to drink?

MR. TRUNDLE 1. I ordered food, actually. To go.

(**BECKY** *reaches down behind the counter and pulls out a brown lunch bag.*)

BECKY 2. Right. You must be Mr. Pickles. I forgot to ask your name when you called.
(*Reading order.*) "Pickles on the side, burger medium-rare, ketchup on one bun, mustard on the other."

MR. TRUNDLE 1. That's me.

BECKY 2. I take it you don't like when the mustard and the ketchup mix together.

MR. TRUNDLE 1. That is correct.

BECKY 2. You do realize once you bite into the...

MR. TRUNDLE 1. No, no, no, let me keep my fantasy.

BECKY 2. Note taken.
(*Extending her hand.*) I'm Becky. The new bartender.

MR. TRUNDLE 1. Ted. Trundle. The new mayor.

BECKY 2. I've heard a lot about you.

MR. TRUNDLE 1. All good, I hope.

BECKY 2. Well...you can't believe everything you hear.

(**MR. TRUNDLE** *mimes pulling out his wallet and handing her money.*)

MR. TRUNDLE 1. You just move to town?

BECKY 2. I grew up here. Just moved back. We have tables. Lots of empty ones, if you want to stay.

MR. TRUNDLE 1. It's probably not a good idea for me to be staring at a wall of liquor right now, but thanks.

> *(He turns to leave.)*

BECKY 2. Mr. Trundle...don't worry about what anyone says. You're going to be a terrific mayor. I can tell.

MR. TRUNDLE 1. I guess that remains to be seen.

> *(He turns to leave again.)*

BECKY 2. Welcome to Popcorn Falls.

MR. TRUNDLE 1. Welcome home.

> *(They look at each other. We see a spark.* **MR. TRUNDLE** *exits with a "Ding-a-ling.")*

[MUSIC NO. 04]

Scene Three: Main Street

(One actor writes "Main Street" on the board. The other sets up two chairs and the small bookshelf. This will become Ms. Parker's living room. **MR. TRUNDLE** *walks in place.* **JOE** *rushes to catch up. They walk in place together.)*

JOE 2. Sorry, Mr. Trundle! Trudy got home from work late so I had to feed the boys.

MR. TRUNDLE 1. Aww, that's sweet.

JOE 2. I tell ya, I am glad we're getting this done now, before we have the babies. How come you never had kids, Mr. Trundle?

MR. TRUNDLE 1. Made other choices.

JOE 2. I don't mean to pry.

MR. TRUNDLE 1. And yet you are.

(They stop walking.)

JOE 2. This is it. Ms. Parker's house.

MR. TRUNDLE 1. That's strange. It looks like the walls inside her house are moving.

JOE 2. Those are cats.

MR. TRUNDLE 1. Cats?! She has that many?! I can't go in there, I have allergies. I won't be able to breathe.

(He makes sound effects of **JOE**'s *phone ringing.)*

JOE 2. Fine, you wait out here and I'll...
(Looking at his phone.) It's Trudy.
(Answering.) What's the matter, honey, what happened, you and the boys okay? They have what? All four of them? That's disgusting!
(Covering phone.) You are so lucky you don't have kids.
(Into phone.) I fed 'em the leftover shrimp quesadilla from Chi Chi's like you told me. I have no idea, I ate the same thing and I don't have dia...

(**MR. TRUNDLE** *makes sound effects of* **JOE**'s
stomach growling.)

Oh. I didn't get dia...

(**MR. TRUNDLE** *continues the growling...it
continues to grow.*)

Oh! Oh my... Honey, I-I-I-I'll be home in a minute!

(*Hangs up.*)

Sorry, Mr. Trundle! I gotta go!

MR. TRUNDLE 1. Wait! What about Ms. Parker?!

JOE 2. Don't have kids, Mr. Trundle! And don't eat at Chi
Chi's!! Ahhh...!

(*He runs off. His yelps of pain turn into a
scream of delight as he runs back on from the
other side of the stage as* **MS. PARKER** *petting
her cat, Mr. Cuddles.* **MR. TRUNDLE** *covers his
face with a handkerchief, trying to lessen the
severity of his cat allergies as he carefully
enters Ms. Parker's bungalow.*)

MS. PARKER 2. ...Ahhh, what glorious news! A theater, right
here in Popcorn Falls! Well, you've certainly come to
the right place.

(*She gives a loud "meow" as she brushes a cat
from a chair. She sits.*)

I know more about theatre than anyone in town.
Except the preacher, of course, but he gravitates toward
the musicals.

(**MR. TRUNDLE** *gives a loud "meow" and "hiss"
as he brushes away a cat, sits.*)

Have you thought of a name for your group?

MR. TRUNDLE 1. Popcorn Community Players.

MS. PARKER 2. PCP! I like it! Oh, but I fear I must decline.
A return to the stage after so many years...

MR. TRUNDLE 1. But Ms. Parker, no one else in this town
knows anything abou...abou... (*Sneezes.*) ...About
theatre. We need your expertise!

MS. PARKER 2. "Expertise," how you flatter!
(Crossing downstage.) Fifteen years as the leading lady of Anchor Bay Players hardly qualifies me as an expert.

MR. TRUNDLE 1. Think of the library!

MS. PARKER 2. *(Transfixed, looking front.)* The library!!

MR. TRUNDLE 1. Your library. Think of the years you've spent transforming it into a thriving institution.

> *(**MS. PARKER** crosses upstage behind **MR. TRUNDLE**.)*

MS. PARKER 2. Still, I couldn't...

MR. TRUNDLE 1. Think of George Washington!

MS. PARKER 2. *(Turning front, again transfixed.)* George!!

> *(Standing behind **MR. TRUNDLE** she manipulates the cat's "tail" to continually hit him in the side of the face. His allergies are now overwhelming.)*

MR. TRUNDLE 1. Imagine him on the front lawn, raising a glass of Popcorn water. Calling his men to battle! A battle to protect innocent Americans...their families... think of the children!

MS. PARKER 2. The children!!

> *(She rushes downstage center. **MR. TRUNDLE** follows.)*

MR. TRUNDLE 1. Every day taking out one of your books that could one day inspire them to fly to the moon! To cure...polio! ...Again! Without you, those dreams will be shattered!

MS. PARKER 2. Over my dead body!

> *(She gives a loud screech as she dumps the cat into **MR. TRUNDLE**'s arms. He can no longer breathe.)*

The ability to read is a God-given right! To feed our souls! We will not let them starve us to death!

MR. TRUNDLE 1. Does that mean you'll do it?

MS. PARKER 2. I have just one query, Mr. Trundle! What play shall we put on first?

MR. TRUNDLE 1. Oh, thank goodness!

> *(He dumps the cat back into* **MS. PARKER**'s *arms, then runs for the door.)*

MS. PARKER 2. Meet me at the library tomorrow's eve. We shall read and ponder, ponder and read and see what "jangles our chain," as they say. All we need now is someone to build our scenery, design the poster, makeup, wigs... "Once more, dear kernels, unto the breach!"

MR. TRUNDLE 1. Tomorrow then, Ms. Parker!

MS. PARKER 2. *(As he exits.)* "Tomorrow – and tomorrow – and tomorrow!"

> *(She takes a dramatic bow, then exits.* **MR. TRUNDLE** *enters; he is back on the street.)*

MR. TRUNDLE 1. Heard you the first time! Ah-Ah-Ah-CHOO!

[MUSIC NO. 05]

> *(***JOE** *grabs the empty bottle of booze from the garbage, then pushes the chairs together to create a bench. He is now* **FLOYD**, *the one-armed lumberyard owner who is very drunk.)*

FLOYD 2.

> IF YOU'RE HAPPY AND YOU KNOW IT, CLAP YOUR HANDS.
>
> *(Claps his hand to his elbow.)*
>
> *(He tries to clap again.* **MR. TRUNDLE** *sneezes.)*

You!

MR. TRUNDLE 1. Floyd.

FLOYD 2. You charlatan! Every penny I had. I bought the wood, the nails, the plywood!

MR. TRUNDLE 1. Not now, Floyd!

FLOYD 2. You promised a housing boom, Mr. Trundle!

MR. TRUNDLE 1. I suggested we build one condo!

FLOYD 2. Thanks to you, I have nothin'!

MR. TRUNDLE 1. You can't blame me, Floyd! I didn't tell you to order a bunch of nails and screws and two-by-fours!

I wouldn't even know what to do with a bunch of nails and screws and... *(Gets idea.)* Scenery! We're going to need scenery! Floyd, I have wonderful news!

> *(He crosses behind **FLOYD** and speaks into his ear.)*

We're opening a theater!

FLOYD 2. A what?

MR. TRUNDLE 1. *(Into his other ear.)* A theater.

FLOYD 2. A what?

> *(**MR. TRUNDLE** sits next to him.)*

MR. TRUNDLE 1. It's something that uses a lot of nails and screws and two-by-fours, and we're going to pay you to build it!

FLOYD 2. You are?! You came through, Mr. Trundle! Hope! Change!
(Offering his half-sawed-off arm.) High five!

MR. TRUNDLE 1. Now we just need to find someone to do the costumes, the posters, the makeup, the wigs...

> *(**FLOYD** does a spit-take.)*

Floyd?

FLOYD 2. No!

MR. TRUNDLE 1. Floyd, what's the matter?

> *(**FLOYD** gets up and looks around the stage.)*

FLOYD 2. Only one person in this town can do all that and wild horses couldn't drag that woman's name through my lips.

MR. TRUNDLE 1. Who is it?

> *(**FLOYD** puts his good arm around **MR. TRUNDLE**'s neck, then pretends to cut him with his other half-arm.)*

FLOYD 2. People cut you, Mr. Trundle! When you're not looking they grab you from behind and cut you like a knife.

MR. TRUNDLE 1. Oh my god, is she the one who...is that what happened to your arm?

FLOYD 2. Some cuts are on the inside. Those hurt the deepest. The ones on the outside...they just make it really hard to put on a sock.

> *(He stumbles off.* **MR. TRUNDLE** *yells after him:)*

MR. TRUNDLE 1. But if you don't tell me her name...!

FLOYD 2. *(Offstage.)* Let dead dogs lie, Mr. Trundle!

MR. TRUNDLE 1. Can't you at least tell me her name?!

[MUSIC NO. 06]

> *(They set the next scene – a table and chair create a middle school classroom.* **MR. TRUNDLE** *sits at a "desk."* **ACTOR 2** *becomes* **MRS. STEPP** *by holding up one hand as if he's smoking. He turns the chalkboard around – written in very large letters: "Mrs. Stepp." School bell.)*

MRS. STEPP 2. *(Underlining her name.)* Mrs. Stepp.

MR. TRUNDLE 1. Your name...it's funny because before you were married you were Miss Stepp. Like, "Oh, I just made a misstep."

MRS. STEPP 2. Don't be so pedestrian. My maiden name was Guided.

MR. TRUNDLE 1. *(Beat.)* Miss Guided.

MRS. STEPP 2. Of the East Nantucket Guideds!

MR. TRUNDLE 1. I was just saying, Mrs. Stepp, that with your artistic and creative abilities...

MRS. STEPP 2. I understand what you're saying. You want to save this town by opening a theater and you need me to build costumes, print the posters, design the wigs, the makeup...well, pass! I've moved on and so should you. Now, as I have a class that starts in five minutes, I would appreciate it if you'd make like a banana – and vamoose!

MR. TRUNDLE 1. Is there anything I can do to...

MRS. STEPP 2. *(Turning her back to him.)* Goodbye, Mr. Trundle.

MR. TRUNDLE 1. It's just that Floyd said... Oh, never mind.

MRS. STEPP 2. *(Quickly turning back.)* Wait! What did Floyd say? Floyd Woodman talked about me? It isn't true. He's a liar! He's mean and cruel and – what did he say?

MR. TRUNDLE 1. Well...actually...he said some really nice things about –

MRS. STEPP 2. I'll do it!

MR. TRUNDLE 1. You will?

*(**MRS. STEPP** saunters over to him.)*

MRS. STEPP 2. Mr. Trundle...do you mind if I call you Edgar?

MR. TRUNDLE 1. My name is Ted.

*(**MRS. STEPP** seductively plays with his tie.)*

MRS. STEPP 2. The next time you have anything to ask me... you'll see I can be very agreeable when asked nicely. *(Grabs his tie, pulling him in close.)* And by nicely, I mean with a glass of Chateauneuf-du-Schlitz and a canister of Pringles.

My only hope is that Floyd doesn't find out about our little... *(Smacking his behind.)* ...menage a deux. He can be a very – jealous – man.

(Tickling his nose.) Voulez-vous faire le Bing Bong avec moi, ce soir? I used to teach ninth-grade French.

MR. TRUNDLE 1. I took Spanish.

MRS. STEPP 2. Adieu, mon amour.

MR. TRUNDLE 1. Adios, amigo.

*(**MRS. STEPP** blows him a kiss. **MR. TRUNDLE** turns away, resisting the urge to throw up.)*

[MUSIC NO. 07]

*(He turns the chalkboard back around and puts a star next to the words "Sudsy Mug." **BECKY** puts on an apron but can't find the lunch bag. **MR. TRUNDLE** throws it to her just in time, then enters with a "Ding-a-ling.")*

Scene Four: Sudsy Mug

(**BECKY** *holds out the brown bag.*)

BECKY 2. Pickles on the side, burger medium-rare, ketchup on one bun, mustard on the other.

MR. TRUNDLE 1. I actually... I think I'll stay, if that's...if you don't mind.

BECKY 2. Let me see if I can find you a table. Oh, look, you can have any of them.

MR. TRUNDLE 1. Gets lonely eating by yourself every night.

(**BECKY** *wipes off the table.* **MR. TRUNDLE** *sits and mimes eating his burger.*)

BECKY 2. How's the mayoring going?

MR. TRUNDLE 1. Fine.

BECKY 2. Have you done this before?

MR. TRUNDLE 1. For a much larger city.

BECKY 2. You wanted something more manageable?

MR. TRUNDLE 1. They didn't give me a choice, actually. How long you been back?

BECKY 2. Little over a week. I moved away to go to acting school. Big dreams of becoming a star.

MR. TRUNDLE 1. Perfect timing. We're opening a theater.

BECKY 2. I gave all that up.

MR. TRUNDLE 1. You gave up your big dream?

BECKY 2. I took a couple courses my one year of college.

MR. TRUNDLE 1. Sounds like you've been gone a lot longer than a year.

BECKY 2. I got...distracted. That's when I... That's when Lydia was born. I had a baby. A girl.

MR. TRUNDLE 1. Lydia would be a very progressive name for a boy.

BECKY 2. She's with my mom right now. We're turning her old sewing room into a princess bedroom. We finally settled on Snow White for the curtains and Sleeping Beauty for the sheets.

(**MR. TRUNDLE** *is staring at her, smiling.*)

BECKY 2. What can I get you to drink?

MR. TRUNDLE 1. Sure you don't want to be part of our acting troupe? "A couple of courses" is a couple more than anyone else has taken.

BECKY 2. I have Coke, Diet Coke and Sprite.

MR. TRUNDLE 1. You see, all we have to do is put on a play and we get to...

BECKY 2. I'd rather not discuss it. If you don't mind.

MR. TRUNDLE 1. Diet Coke, please.

(*Uncomfortable silence as* **BECKY** *pours a Diet Coke, doing the sound effects of the fountain gun...clearly it's a large glass. She gives it one extra squirt, then carries it to* **MR. TRUNDLE**.)

BECKY 2. Sometimes I feel like Humpty Dumpty. Trying to put the scrambled pieces of my life back together.

MR. TRUNDLE 1. For the record...I prefer my eggs scrambled.

BECKY 2. Note taken.

[MUSIC NO. 08]

Scene Five: Mr. Doyle's Office

(**MR. TRUNDLE** *writes "Doyle's Office" on the board.* **ACTOR 2** *sets up the office, stands behind the desk, and becomes* **MR. DOYLE**. **MR. TRUNDLE** *is holding the white envelope.*)

MR. DOYLE 2. You did what?!

MR. TRUNDLE 1. I informed the Cattaraugus Arts Council that we will indeed be using these funds.

MR. DOYLE 2. You will never see that money.

MR. TRUNDLE 1. They assured me we will receive the check immediately after our first performance.
(*Holding out the contract.*) All we need now is for you to sign this contract.

MR. DOYLE 2. What do you know about opening a theater, Mr. Trundle?

MR. TRUNDLE 1. We've pooled our resources.

MR. DOYLE 2. You don't have any resources.

(*He mimes pouring himself a glass of water.*)

You don't even have water.

(*He glugs down the water.*)

MR. TRUNDLE 1. We have a very determined group of people.

(**MR. DOYLE** *puts down his water with a satisfied "Ahh."*)

MR. DOYLE 2. Let me give you a more accurate list of your assets. You have one drinking establishment, a Suzy's Donut Shop, a gas station slash pizza parlor slash nail salon...

MR. TRUNDLE 1. ...Slash sushi, they've expanded.

MR. DOYLE 2. And one blinking yellow light.

MR. TRUNDLE 1. Yeah, that's pretty sad.

MR. DOYLE 2. You were fired from your last post, am I correct?

MR. TRUNDLE 1. You know perfectly well what happened.

MR. DOYLE 2. Technically, they couldn't fire you for alcoholism.

MR. TRUNDLE 1. What they did was against the law.

MR. DOYLE 2. And did you fight the charges?

(No answer.)

So you found your way here – to the Island of Misfit Toys. All that's left in Popcorn Falls are the parched kernels too apathetic to pop from the pan.

MR. TRUNDLE 1. That's an awful lot of P-popping just to prove a point, pal!

MR. DOYLE 2. Popcorn Falls is dead, Mr. Trundle. I suggest you pack up your little theater and find yourself a new town.

(Pushing the intercom button, he says, "Beep.")

Miss Brown, tell Mr. Green I'm on my way.

MR. TRUNDLE 1. You can't do this, Mr. Doyle!

MR. DOYLE 2. Good day, Mr. Trundle.

(He starts off but is stopped by:)

MR. TRUNDLE 1. Everyone will hate you!

(Luring him in.) You're forgetting something very important, Mr. Doyle. The people of Popcorn Falls will soon be citizens of Cattaraugus and have the right to vote for all public offices. If you don't let them put on a play, if you take away the one chance they have of saving themselves...they will hate you. On the other hand, if you give us time...allow *me* to be the failure, it's me they will hate. You can sue me, throw me in jail for misappropriation of funds. And you, Mr. Doyle, you will become their hero. Don't underestimate the people of Popcorn Falls, Mr. Doyle. They are fighters. Like George Washington.

(Holding out contract.) Now if you will please sign this contract, I have play practice!

> *(**MR. DOYLE** turns to **MR. TRUNDLE**, gives short, patronizing applause, gets an idea, grabs the contract, and returns to his desk. He writes on the contract.)*

MR. DOYLE 2. Tomorrow! You need to put on your play by tomorrow.

MR. TRUNDLE 1. What?!

MR. DOYLE 2. The grant was awarded without an end date. I've just added one.

MR. TRUNDLE 1. We can't put on a play in one day!

> (**MR. DOYLE** *holds up the contract as if to rip it in half.*)

MR. DOYLE 2. Oh, well. Too bad.

MR. TRUNDLE 1. One month!

MR. DOYLE 2. Two days!

MR. TRUNDLE 1. Three weeks!

MR. DOYLE 2. Four days!

MR. TRUNDLE 1. Five weeks!

MR. DOYLE 2. Six weeks!

MR. TRUNDLE 1. Seven days!

MR. DOYLE 2. Perfect!!

MR. TRUNDLE 1. *(Banging his palm on his forehead.)* D'oh!

MR. DOYLE 2. One week.

> *(He writes on the contract.)*

If there is no play in exactly seven days and, let's see... *(Looking at his watch.)* It's 7:59, I'll even throw in a minute. You have until eight p.m., one week from tonight, to put on your play. Or I will see that you rot in jail.

(Presenting contract.) Do we have a deal?

> (**MR. TRUNDLE** *reluctantly takes the contract.*)

S-s-plendid. Oh, and you've just sold your first ticket. I'll be standing in the back...next to the authorities.

> *(He exits with a maniacal laugh.* **MR. TRUNDLE** *crosses to the desk, picks up the envelope, and slowly inserts the contract.* **MR. DOYLE** *pops back in from another entrance, scaring* **MR. TRUNDLE.**)

MR. DOYLE 2. Six days, twenty-three hours and fifty-eight minutes!

(He gives a loud cackle, then exits.)

[MUSIC NO. 09]

Scene Six: Library

(**MR. TRUNDLE** *writes "Library" on the board.*
JOE *turns the counter around so it is now
a bookshelf in the library.* **JOE** *is hanging
upside down on a chair, moaning. They are
exhausted, having been up all night reading
plays.* **MR. TRUNDLE** *sits, reading.* **JOE**'s
moaning grows louder.)

MR. TRUNDLE 1. I'm trying to read, Joe! Joe, will you stop!

JOE 2. Why did you have to say we could put on a play in a
week? Why didn't you say two weeks, three weeks?

MR. TRUNDLE 1. I was under a lot of pressure!

JOE 2. Yeah, well so am I!

(*Crawling off chair.*) I'm going home.

MR. TRUNDLE 1. Keep reading.

JOE 2. I need sleep!

MR. TRUNDLE 1. I can't do this by myself. There must be
ONE play you liked!

JOE 2. (*Holding up a play.*) We got hundreds of angry men,
how are we gonna pick just twelve?!

(*Holds up another play.*) Where was the streetcar?!

(*Another play.*) Where were the cherries?

(*Another play.*) And who puts raisins in the sun –
they're already dry!

(*He stands.*)

MR. TRUNDLE 1. Will you quit fooling around! This doesn't
work, who winds up in jail? Me! So I would appreciate
it if you sat here – quietly, and we will read all these
plays – again!

(*In the blink of an eye,* **JOE** *becomes* **MS.
PARKER**, *popping up on the other side of* **MR.
TRUNDLE**.)

MS. PARKER 2. We'll write our own play!

MR. TRUNDLE 1. Ms. Parker!

MS. PARKER 2. Of course. Why didn't I think of this before?!

> (**MR. TRUNDLE** *sneaks a book behind his back.*)

MR. TRUNDLE 1. That's ridiculous. Ms. Parker, we can't write a play!

JOE 2. We wouldn't know the first thing.

> (**MS. PARKER** *grabs the book from behind* **MR. TRUNDLE***'s back.*)

MS. PARKER 2. Here we are...

> (*Blowing dust off the book, presenting it to the boys.*)

Everything You Wanted to Know About Theatre. My very own copy signed by my drama teacher, Mr. Ray Harrington.

(*Handing* **MR. TRUNDLE** *the book.*) This will tell you everything you need to know.

MR. TRUNDLE 1. (*Reading.*) "A playwright has the ability to shift an audience's perspective, move mountains with words, and thereby change the world."

MS. PARKER 2. Poetry.

MR. TRUNDLE 1. How long will it take us to write a play? Can we do it in a couple days?

MS. PARKER 2. Shakespeare wrote nearly fifty in his short lifetime. Lorca, over two thousand.

MR. TRUNDLE 1. Two thousand?!

(*To* **JOE**.) We put our heads together, we should be able to come up with *one*. Where do we start, Ms. Parker?

MS. PARKER 2. Stanislavski always wrote for his troupe of actors. I think it's time to explore the talent of Popcorn Falls!

> **[MUSIC NO. 10]**
>
> (*A [pre-recorded]* **RADIO DJ** *speaks as* **MR. TRUNDLE** *writes "Tryouts" on the board. They both listen with excitement hearing Mr. Trundle's voice on the radio.*)

Scene Seven: Tryouts

RADIO DJ 2. *(Pre-recorded.)* This is Little Johnny Neudeck, with WPOP! Tryouts are being held tomorrow. All interested are asked to show up with a monologue of their choice. Mr. Trundle, maybe you can explain what a monologue is.

MR. TRUNDLE 1. *(Pre-recorded.)* Well, it's when one person talks for a long time and the other person doesn't listen.

RADIO DJ 2. *(Pre-recorded.)* A lot of talking and no listening... I call that a marriage.

> *(Laughs at his own joke.)*

So come on down to the town hall and show off your talent.

> **(MR. TRUNDLE 1** *becomes* **HANS,** *wearing a monocle and speaking with a heavy German accent.)*

HANS 1. I pledge allegiance to ze flag of ze United States of America...oond to ze Republic, for richard stands, voon nation, oonder God, indivisible, viz liberty oond justice for all.

> *(He bows.)*

JOE 2. That was really something, Hans. Did you bring a *comic* monologue?

HANS 1. Zat vas my comic monologue.

JOE 2. That's all we need to see.

HANS 1. Scheisse!

JOE 2. *(As* **HANS** *exits.)* My best to everyone at the funeral home!

HANS 1. *(Offstage.)* Yah, yah!

> **(MR. TRUNDLE** *sneaks on, joining* **JOE** *at the table.)*

JOE 2. *(Referring to Hans.)* You should see that guy's work.

MR. TRUNDLE 1. You've seen him act?

JOE 2. He's a mortician. Dolled up my aunt with a roll of duct tape and a Sharpie, made her look twenty years younger.

> (**MR. TRUNDLE** and **JOE** get a brilliant idea at the same time.)

JOE 2 & MR. TRUNDLE 1. Makeup!

> (**JOE** exits to become **MARGIE**, the ultimate millennial-in-training. She speaks "Valley-speak" and is continually scrolling on her cell phone.)

MR. TRUNDLE 1. See? What did I tell you? Putting on a play is a piece of cake! Okay...who do we have next?

MARGIE 2. Hi...

MR. TRUNDLE 1. Good afternoon... (Looking at the paper.) Margie.

MARGIE 2. Hi. Is this America's Got Talent? I want to be on America's Got Talent.

MR. TRUNDLE 1. You do?

MARGIE 2. (Resting her arm on her head.) Obviously.

MR. TRUNDLE 1. We're looking for actors to be in our play. Did you bring a monologue?

MARGIE 2. A what?

MR. TRUNDLE 1. A monologue.

MARGIE 2. A what?

MR. TRUNDLE 1. We wrote the requirements on the flyer. Did you read the flyer?

MARGIE 2. The one outside?

MR. TRUNDLE 1. Yes.

MARGIE 2. The one on the telephone pole?

MR. TRUNDLE 1. Yes.

MARGIE 2. The purple one?

MR. TRUNDLE 1. Yes.

MARGIE 2. No.

> (She takes a selfie.)

MR. TRUNDLE 1. No, you didn't read it?

MARGIE 2. Is acting when you cry?

MR. TRUNDLE 1. *(Looks to "Joe," then.)* Yes. Yes, it is.

MARGIE 2. Because I cry all the time. Does that make me a good actress?

MR. TRUNDLE 1. I don't know. Can you cry right now?

MARGIE 2. Can you tell me something sad?

MR. TRUNDLE 1. Maybe you should think of something yourself...in your head.

> *(**MARGIE** looks front, making a peculiar face.)*

Are you thinking?

> *(**MARGIE** begins to laugh.)*

MARGIE 2. I was thinking of something sad, but then it got funny. My mother lost three fingers in the garbage disposal...

MR. TRUNDLE 1. *(Jumping from chair and leading her offstage.)* Okay! That's all we need to see! Thank you! Love the piercings!

> *(He exits as **JOE** steps forward. The ninety-three-year-old **MR. UPMALL** slowly shuffles onstage.)*

JOE 2. Thank you all for auditioning today. We had no idea your talent would be at that level.

MR. UPMALL 1. Tinkle!

JOE 2. Rehearsals will take place in the warehouse at Floyd's Lumberyard. This way we can practice while the scenery is being built.

MR. UPMALL 1. Tinkle!

JOE 2. The bathroom's down the hall, Mr. Upmall.

MR. UPMALL 1. Tinkle the ivories! I'm here to audition!

JOE 2. First of all, we don't have a piano...

MR. UPMALL 1. That's okay, I'm deaf!

JOE 2. Mr. Upmall, the auditions were from two to four.

MR. UPMALL 1. I started walking here at a quarter to one.

JOE 2. Well...

MR. UPMALL 1. Yesterday.

JOE 2. Well, that's...

MR. UPMALL 1. I hit traffic. I got stuck behind a parked car.

JOE 2. Whenever you're ready, Mr. Upmall.

MR. UPMALL 1. Ready? I've been waiting for this moment all my life!

> *(Throws down his cane.)*

A-five, six, seven, eight!

> *(He takes a deep breath, then clutches his heart, slowly collapsing to the ground in a long, drawn-out comic death scene. He finally looks dead.)*

JOE 2. Mr. Upmall? Mr. Upmall, are you okay?

> *(**MR. UPMALL** pops up, a big smile.)*

MR. UPMALL 1. Acting!! Ha-ha!
> *(To **JOE**.)* Did I get the part?!

JOE 2. You're hired!

MR. UPMALL 1. Yay!
> *(Clutching his chest.)* Uh-oh!

> *(He falls back, his legs in the air. Lights change quickly to the Sudsy Mug.)*

Scene Eight: Sudsy Mug

(JOE ties the shirt/apron around his waist to become BECKY.)

BECKY 2. You're making that up!

(MR. UPMALL becomes MR. TRUNDLE. Together, he and BECKY set up the Sudsy Mug.)

MR. TRUNDLE 1. I kid you not! He was lying on the floor like this for hours. Doc says he'll be fine. Apparently he's like one of those goats on YouTube – falls over whenever he gets excited. Listen, I promised myself I wouldn't ask again but is there any way you'd want to be part of our troupe?

BECKY 2. You don't need me. You have Joe.

MR. TRUNDLE 1. Joe? Our Joe?

BECKY 2. He never told you?

MR. TRUNDLE 1. Told me what?

BECKY 2. He was the class clown. He could imitate the teachers, our friends. He even does a mean Becky Zarna.

(No reaction from MR. TRUNDLE.)

That's me. My last name is Zarna.

MR. TRUNDLE 1. Oh, sorry.

(As they continue, MR. TRUNDLE sits, BECKY places the lunch bag on the table. They both mime eating fries as they talk.)

BECKY 2. One time... I was so nervous... I was auditioning for an acting scholarship for a college...and Joe was sitting in the hall waiting with me. And he started... oh my god...he started pretending to be all these celebrities stopping by to wish me luck. He was Arnold Schwarzenegger. He was Christopher Walken, Carol Channing...

MR. TRUNDLE 1. Seriously?

BECKY 2. I couldn't be nervous if I tried! I told him the only way I would go away to acting school is if he went with me. So that was our big plan. He'd become a comedian and I would be the serious actor.

MR. TRUNDLE 1. He's never said a word.

BECKY 2. We'd end up in New York. Or LA. Somewhere glamorous like that.

MR. TRUNDLE 1. What happened?

BECKY 2. He literally left me waiting for him at the bus stop.

MR. TRUNDLE 1. That doesn't sound like Joe.

BECKY 2. I kept writing him. Telling him where I was. It all worked out for the best. Trudy always had a thing for Joe.

(Looking at her watch.) Lydia's bedtime. I have to call her so she can tell me a bedtime story.

> *(She exits into the kitchen.* **MR. TRUNDLE** *yells after her.)*

MR. TRUNDLE 1. Becky! I'm going to use the little boy's room. I'm not leaving! Don't throw away my fries!

> *(***JOE*** *enters the Sudsy Mug with a "Ding-a-ling." He's been standing at the door, overhearing.)*

Joe! I was just about to call you. Ms. Parker's book – Amazing. Everything we need to know. Help yourself to some fries.

(Heading to the bathroom.) Too much Diet Coke.

> *(He heads off to the bathroom.* **JOE** *sits, eats a french fry, and looks at the book.* **BECKY** *comes back from the kitchen wearing the same apron, adorably tucking her hair behind her ear.)*

BECKY 1. She sang to me! It was either "Three Blind Mice" or "It's Raining Men."

JOE 2. The fries are good.

> *(***BECKY*** *turns to see* **JOE**.*)*

BECKY 1. Joe.

JOE 2. Becky. You're back. You could have called.

BECKY 1. I did call. And I wrote, many times.

JOE 2. I meant now.

BECKY 1. I know what you meant. I understand you and Trudy got married. That's good. You have four kids.

JOE 2. Two sets of twins. Another set on the way.

BECKY 1. Twins are good luck.

JOE 2. Yeah? I should've bought a lottery ticket.

BECKY 1. Look, let's just… You decided you wanted to stay here. There's no crime in that.

JOE 2. I thought about you. Did *you*?

BECKY 1. You left me standing at a bus stop. I think about that sometimes. Excuse me. I have to go…marry the ketchups.

>   (**BECKY** *exits.* **JOE** *takes a step toward the kitchen.*)

JOE 2. Becks…

>   (*He turns to go as* **MR. TRUNDLE** *re-enters from the bathroom.*)

MR. TRUNDLE 1. Hold on, Joe. Joe…we can do this.
(*Holding up the book.*) We can write a play. All we need is a protagonist and an antagonist.

JOE 2. Uh-huh.

MR. TRUNDLE 1. That's a good guy and a bad guy. And the good guy has to want something *really* bad. And the bad guy, he has to stop him from getting it. And if the good guy gets what he wants, it's a happy ending and if he doesn't get what he wants, it's a sad ending. Example. I want this hamburger. You stop me from getting it. It's a play! Simple.

JOE 2. So, you're the good guy and you want Becky?

MR. TRUNDLE 1. What?

JOE 2. And I'm the bad guy getting in your way?

MR. TRUNDLE 1. What? Joe. No. Joe, I don't know what you thought was going on.

JOE 2. Looks like you two are having a good time, that's all.

MR. TRUNDLE 1. She's a good person. I like hamburgers. We laugh. Joe, I had no idea. I mean, Trudy, the kids.

JOE 2. No, it's cool. Old tapes running in my head. Surprised me to see her, is all.

MR. TRUNDLE 1. Okay. I'm going to stop home. I'll meet you at the lumberyard. All we have to do now is come up with a story.

(He turns to go, then stops.)

Joe... Becky and me – If I thought for one second...

JOE 2. *(Laughing.)* Stop. It's fine. All cool. Go. See you at the lumberyard.

*(**MR. TRUNDLE** exits, "Ding-a-ling." **JOE** takes a beat.)*

[MUSIC NO. 11]

Scene Nine: Lumberyard

(MR. TRUNDLE writes "Lumberyard" on the board as ACTOR 2 sets up two chairs, one on either side of the board, facing center.)

MR. TRUNDLE 1. Okay, everyone! Now that we're cast, we have two days to write our play. That will leave us three days to rehearse, build the sets, costumes, posters – plenty of time.

(Looks at his watch.) Joe must be running late so why don't we get started?

(Refers to book.) First things first...a title. We need to find a title for our play. And this title doesn't even have to make sense. *A Lion in Winter. The Glass Menagerie. The Elephant Man.* These titles mean nothing. What should we call our play?

(Looks around room.)

Floyd?

FLOYD 2. I got nothin'!

(MR. TRUNDLE speaks to an empty chair as ACTOR 2 moves his chair to become MARGIE.)

MR. TRUNDLE 1. Hans? ...Anything? Margie?

MARGIE 2. What about...*The Play.*

MR. TRUNDLE 1. *The Play*! I like it.

(Writes "The Play" on the board.)

Thank you, Margie. Nice and simple.

(Turns to group.) This is coming together fast. Now, who has an idea for what our play might be about?

(Reads from book.) The book says, "Write what you know." Ahhh. What do we know? Does anyone know anything? About anything?

(He sits and puts on a monocle to become HANS.)

HANS 1. I know about Fred und Ginger. Ven I vas very small my grandfather vould sit me on his lap and ve vould do the "bouncy-bouncy" and ve vould vatch ze American dance movies.

"NACHT UND TAG...YOU ARE ZE FUN."

Zat is vhy I come to America. Everything here is happy endings. Zis is vhy I vork viz ze dead people. I give zem a happy ending in ze casket.

(He jumps up from the chair.)

MR. TRUNDLE 1. A happy ending! I like it. I love it! Gives us something to work towards!

(Writes "Happy Ending" on the board.)

A happy ending. Now, we're cooking with gas! Any other ideas?

*(He moves a chair in place. **ACTOR 2** sits and becomes **MS. PARKER**.)*

MS. PARKER 2. Kittens.

MR. TRUNDLE 1. A kitten!

(Writes "Kitten" on the board.)

Our play could be about a kitten.

MS. PARKER 2. An adorable little kitten who is taken to the ASPCA.

(Turning to Hans.) Ja?

MR. TRUNDLE 1. I smell a happy ending!

(Writes "ASPCA" on the board.)

MS. PARKER 2. Except it's not the ASPCA. It's a front for a company that takes kittens and stuffs them through a meat grinder and minces them into dog food.

MR. TRUNDLE 1. Well that took a turn.

MS. PARKER 2. But she runs away just in time!

MR. TRUNDLE 1. And we're back to happy!

*(He jumps in chair to become **HANS**.)*

HANS 1. Perhaps ze kitten could find love in ze arms of a pirate!

FLOYD 2. I could play the pirate.

MRS. STEPP 2. He said "arms" plural!

MR. TRUNDLE 1. A pirate!

> *(He writes "Pirate" on the board.* **MRS. STEPP** *approaches.)*

MRS. STEPP 2. We need a love story! Where two people fall in love.

MR. TRUNDLE 1. *(Writing on board.)* "Love story."

MRS. STEPP 2. You look like you enjoy a good love story, Mr. Trundle. Two consenting adults meeting in the art supply closet.

> *(She wraps her arms and legs around him seductively.)*

MR. TRUNDLE 1. Anyone else?

MRS. STEPP 2. Twisting themselves into a mind-blowing orgasmic pretzel.

MR. TRUNDLE 1. Anyone at all?

MRS. STEPP 2. Do you like pretzels, Mr. Trundle?

FLOYD 2. I'll tell you what this play should be about! A strapping young upstart who builds sculptures from wood and plaster until a freak accident involving a telephone pole and a Mexican stripper forces him to abandon his dreams and open a lumberyard in a shit-hole town no one's ever heard of.

MRS. STEPP 2. Does that give him license to break a promise he made twenty years ago?!

FLOYD 2. It does when the promise was made up in someone's head!

MR. TRUNDLE 1. Okay...

MRS. STEPP 2. *(Forcing Floyd back in his chair.)* One more crack out-a-you and I'll pay a hooker to saw off your other arm!!

MR. TRUNDLE 1. Stop!

> *(He runs around setting up the Sudsy Mug.)*

MR. TRUNDLE 1. Now...here is what I am going to do... I will take all our ideas... I will jumble them all up in my head...and I will write the play myself. Okay?

*(The group [*ACTOR 2*] exits, mumbling to each other.)*

MRS. STEPP 2. Grumble, grumble, rhubarb, rhubarb.

MR. TRUNDLE 1. Play practice is over. Thank you.

*(He is finally alone. **MR. DOYLE** appears.)*

MR. DOYLE 2. Three days, two hours and one minute!

(Maniacal laugh.)

[MUSIC NO. 12]

Scene Ten: Sudsy Mug

(**MR. TRUNDLE** *erases the board and tries to get out of the room but is stopped by* **AUSTIN**.)

AUSTIN 2. Mayor Trundle. Mayor Trundle, if I may?

MR. TRUNDLE 1. What seems to be the problem, officer?

AUSTIN 2. I could be at home eating dinner, watching TV, sitting on the pot reading the paper, you know what I'm thinking about?

MR. TRUNDLE 1. Do I want to know?

AUSTIN 2. The safety of Popcorn Falls.

MR. TRUNDLE 1. That's reassuring. Now, if you'll excuse me.

(*He grabs his book and script, tries to leave.* **AUSTIN** *blocks him.*)

AUSTIN 2. I need you to fight for me, Mr. Trundle. I need you to talk to Mr. Doyle.

MR. TRUNDLE 1. About what?

AUSTIN 2. My daddy was chief of police, and his daddy, and his daddy!

MR. TRUNDLE 1. (*Crossing downstage.*) Austin...

AUSTIN 2. It's in my blood!

MR. TRUNDLE 1. Mr. Doyle does not care what I think.

AUSTIN 2. My mama will be so disappointed!

MR. TRUNDLE 1. (*Frustrated.*) Austin, being Chief of Police of a large city is much harder than being the deputy of Popcorn Falls. Sometimes we have to recognize our own limitations. I'm sorry.

(*He walks away.* **AUSTIN** *talks into his "walkie-talkie/stun gun."*)

AUSTIN 2. I tried, Mama... I tried.

(*He lowers his face in shame...accidentally zapping his face with the stun gun.*)

Ow!

[MUSIC NO. 13]

(**MR. TRUNDLE** *sets up the Sudsy Mug, then sits. He turns the other chair so it's facing upstage. He grabs the few crumpled papers from the trash can and throws them under the table, then sits, rips a page from his pad, and throws it on the floor.* **ACTOR 2** *emerges from the kitchen, bent over, wearing the apron shirt backwards so it looks like a dress. He is now* **LYDIA,** *Becky's young daughter, bringing* **MR. TRUNDLE** *his Diet Coke.* **LYDIA** *sits on the chair that is facing upstage and drapes the shirt over the back so it looks like a dress.*

LYDIA 2. Here's your Diet Coke, Mr. Pickles.

MR. TRUNDLE 1. Thank you, Lydia, that's very kind of you.

LYDIA 2. My mom's in the kitchen. She said I should bring this to you so you don't drink anything stronger. Wha... what are you drawing?

MR. TRUNDLE 1. I'm not actually...well, what I'm *trying* to draw is...a world, I guess.

LYDIA 2. W-w-what kind of world?

MR. TRUNDLE 1. A perfect world where everything works out and everyone ends up happy.

LYDIA 2. Are you happy?

MR. TRUNDLE 1. Sure.

LYDIA 2. How come you look so sad?

MR. TRUNDLE 1. That's just my face. Because I'm an adult.

LYDIA 2. How come?

MR. TRUNDLE 1. Because I'm drawing a world I know nothing about.

LYDIA 2. Sometimes, when I'm scared, I sleep in my mom's bed, and then sometimes we draw beautiful pictures, and then I'm not scared anymore.

MR. TRUNDLE 1. Aw, that's lovely.

LYDIA 2. Maybe you should sleep with my mom and she can help you make something beautiful.

MR. TRUNDLE 1. That's very good advice. Okay, better get back to work. Oops, I think I heard your mom calling you.

LYDIA 2. *(Leaving.)* Bye, Mr. Pickles! Don't forget what I said about sleeping with my mom.

MR. TRUNDLE 1. Yep. Nope. Got it, right here.
(Pointing to his temple.) Locked in.

> **(LYDIA** *exits into the kitchen.)*

Thanks again for my Diet Coke!

> **(BECKY** *comes out of the kitchen, tying the apron around her waist, turning back to speak to Lydia.)*

BECKY 2. Lydia, honey, Grandma is waiting for you at the back door. I'll call you in an hour to say goodnight.
(Notices the wads of paper on the floor.) Look at this mess.
(Calls back into the kitchen.) Lydia, you get back here right now!

MR. TRUNDLE 1. No, no, no...that's all me.

> *(Picks up his papers.)*

Becky...

BECKY 2. Yes?

MR. TRUNDLE 1. I have a confession to make.

BECKY 2. Yes?

MR. TRUNDLE 1. I hate theatre!

BECKY 2. No, you don't.

MR. TRUNDLE 1. I do.

BECKY 2. How can you hate theatre?

MR. TRUNDLE 1. It's not that hard, really.

BECKY 2. What's the last play you saw?

MR. TRUNDLE 1. *(Tries hard to remember.)* The tour of... *Jacob and His Exciting Multicolored Raincoat?*

BECKY 2. Oh, dear god!

MR. TRUNDLE 1. What? What am I missing? What am I not getting?

BECKY 2. Okay. There was this time... I must have been fourteen. We were on a field trip and they stuck us all in this auditorium to watch *Romiette and Julio*. A rock version of *Romeo and Juliet*.

MR. TRUNDLE 1. Ugh.

BECKY 2. It was worse than "Ugh." It was boring and annoying, and so loud we couldn't understand what anyone was saying. And to top it all off, this girl I despised, Karen Collier, was sitting behind me kicking my chair, trying to annoy me. Suddenly, in the middle of the show, the entire theater goes black. So they make everyone go outside and wait at the back of the school on these hills. Well, they weren't exactly hills... I'm not sure why I feel I need to tell you every tiny detail.

MR. TRUNDLE 1. *(Indicating for her to sit.)* Please.

BECKY 2. So after about fifteen minutes, one of the actors starts singing. Pretty soon *all* the actors are singing. They perform the entire show for us. No sets. No costumes. And by the end of it, I look over, and Karen Collier is smiling at me. And on the bus ride back, she sits next to me and we talk the whole ride home about the play. How cute the guy was playing Julio. How sad it was at the end when they died. A girl who hadn't spoken to me since kindergarten. And I remember thinking to myself...wouldn't I be the luckiest person in the world if I could be a part of something that brought people together like this? To share an experience that has never happened before, and will never happen again?

> *(She finally looks over at* **MR. TRUNDLE**, *who, over the course of the story, has fallen head over heels in love with her.)*

What? Why are you looking at me like that? What?

MR. TRUNDLE 1. I'm married. Divorced. Getting a divorce. Marilyn and I were married fourteen years.

BECKY 2. You don't have to...

MR. TRUNDLE 1. No, let me... Jeffrey Cooper. He was my Karen Collier. My rival in the last town. I beat him by a landslide. Highest approval rating of any mayor. You know when you really own something? You're right where you belong, you're skimming across the top of the water. And I was good, Becky. I was a great mayor. Then one day I notice Marilyn's phone ring and it says "JC," and I'm thinking...well, I know she's not getting a a butt dial from Jesus Christ. So I follow her one night, to her mother's. Only it wasn't her mother's.

BECKY 2. Jeffrey Cooper?

MR. TRUNDLE 1. I started drinking...again. And then I got... *(Using Becky's words.)* ...distracted. I did something... I made a very, very bad decision for the town. After I resigned, Jeffrey Cooper swept in. And here's the kicker. He then proceeded to dump Marilyn, calling her an "entitled social climber." I crawled out of town on the next train. That's my story.

BECKY 2. I kind of guessed. About the divorce part. It's something you notice as a bartender. Single men drink beer, married men drink hard liquor, divorced men drink diet soda.

MR. TRUNDLE 1. Is that true?

BECKY 2. No. But it got you to smile. You're lovely with words.

MR. TRUNDLE 1. I should get over to the lumberyard.

> *(Stands to leave.)*

Romiette and Julio, huh? Thanks for telling me that story.

BECKY 2. May your mustard and ketchup remain forever separated.

MR. TRUNDLE 1. Yours too.

BECKY 2. Well, look at that. I got you to smile twice.

> *(**MR. TRUNDLE** exits with a big smile and a "Ding-a-ling.")*

[MUSIC NO. 14]

Scene Eleven: First Rehearsal

(**MR. TRUNDLE** *writes "Lumberyard" on the board.* **ACTOR 2** *sets both chairs facing upstage.*)

[Note: In this scene the actors can continually cross in front of each other to facilitate character changes.]

MR. TRUNDLE 1. Quiet! Quiet, everyone!

Welcome to our first rehearsal.

(Refers to the book.) As Shakespeare once said, "The play's the thing!" We will now rehearse – our thing. We start with Joe, our narrator. He enters and... Is Joe... has anyone seen Joe?

MRS. STEPP 2. *(Standing.)* Too bad we don't have an understudy.

HANS 1. I already know his lines!

MRS. STEPP 2. You do?

HANS 1. Ja! I have a photographic...vat's the vord...

MRS. STEPP 2. Memory?

HANS 1. Zat's the vun!

MRS. STEPP 2. *(Crossing HANS.)* Oy gevalt.

MR. TRUNDLE 1. Perfect! Then places, everyone!

(Handing her the script.) Ms. Parker, if you don't mind.

MS. PARKER 2. Thank you, Mr. Trundle. The great work begins!

HANS 1. *(Addressing audience, reciting like a poem.)* Ladies und gentlemen, velcome to our show. Zere is the door, but ve hope you vill not go. Our story today, ve hope you are smitten. It centers around an adorable cat.

MS. PARKER 2. *(Correcting him.)* Kitten!

HANS 1. Kitten! Scheisse!

(**MS. PARKER** *crosses downstage center. She speaks in "cat."*)

MS. PARKER 2. Meow, Meow, Meow, MEOW, MEOW, MEOW!!

MR. TRUNDLE 1. Ms. Parker?! Ms. Parker, what are you doing? You're supposed to be saying the lines.

MS. PARKER 2. Kittens don't speak English and nor shall I. The audience will know what I'm saying by my subtle arm movements and suggestive winks. It's called acting.

MR. TRUNDLE 1. Mmmm-okay.

(Crossing her.) And then, enter...

> *(**MRS. STEPP** steps forward, reading script.)*

MRS. STEPP 2. "Alms for the poor. Alms for the poor. A nun's work is never done."

*(To **MR. TRUNDLE**.)* Jesus Christ, you made me the Mother Superior?!

MR. TRUNDLE 1. An actor's job is to stretch. Proceed.

MRS. STEPP 2. *(Reading.)* Oh, look, a kitten! Why don't I take you to the ASPCA where they will find you a nice home? God willing they don't put you to sleep.

MR. TRUNDLE 1. Perfect! Now, the set of the ASPCA is pushed on by Joe...who is still not here.

*(Crossing **MRS. STEPP**.)* Has anyone talked to Joe?

FLOYD 2. Can we cut to my part? My glue's almost dry and I can't make heads or tails of this stupid script anyway.

> *(Shoving the script into **MR. TRUNDLE**'s hand.)*

MR. TRUNDLE 1. Okay everyone, we will skip to the top of page ten where the pirate enters.

FLOYD 2. Who cares when I enter? I want my money!

MR. TRUNDLE 1. As soon as we put on the play.

FLOYD 2. You have any idea how much this play of yours is costing me? Do you know what I've spent on insulation alone?!

MR. TRUNDLE 1. You insulated the walls of the scenery?

FLOYD 2. You said, "Make it real."

MR. TRUNDLE 1. I said make it *look* real.

FLOYD 2. All that work for nothin'! No one's going to come to this stupid thing anyway!

(**ACTOR 2** *pops out from behind* **MR. TRUNDLE.**)

MRS. STEPP 2. Oh, yes they will! I have threatened to flunk every child in my class if I don't see their parents' butts in the front row. THAT is how you fill an audience, NOT by shoving insulation between two pieces of dry rot!

(**ACTOR 2** *pops out from the other side of* **MR. TRUNDLE.**)

FLOYD 2. The only dry rot I see is between your...

MR. TRUNDLE 1. (*Stepping between them.*) Okay! Top of page ten. The pirate and...

(*Handing* **MS. PARKER** *the script.*) ...The *kitten* are alone...

MS. PARKER 2. MEOW! MEOW!

MR. TRUNDLE 1. She is still speaking "cat."

(*Crossing in front of* **FLOYD.**)

FLOYD 2. (*Jumping into his role, reading from the script.*) "Arrr! Holding your face in my two strong hands..."

MR. TRUNDLE 1. Quick rewrite!

(*He grabs the script, "rewrites," hands it back.*)

FLOYD 2. (*Reading rewrite.*) "Arrr! Holding your face in my *one* strong hand."

MRS. STEPP 2. Hold it! Hold it! Do I have to say "pentecostal" three times in one sentence? Can I cut one of these?

MR. TRUNDLE 1. Cut whatever you want.

MRS. STEPP 2. Don't say that while I'm looking at Floyd's only good arm.

MR. TRUNDLE 1. Can we please just get through the script?!

(**ACTOR 2** *jumps into a chair to be* **MARGIE.**)

MARGIE 2. Can my character chew gum?

MR. TRUNDLE 1. You're playing a tree.

MARGIE 2. I thought I was playing the raccoon.

MR. TRUNDLE 1. What raccoon?

> *(Taking script from **MARGIE**.)*

There's no raccoon in this play.

MARGIE 2. *(Gets up, jumps around imitating a raccoon.)* I want to play a raccoon! I want to play a raccoon!!

> **(MR. TRUNDLE** *addresses the audience.* **ACTOR 2** *stands behind him, popping out as each character.)*

MR. TRUNDLE 1. Okay, listen up everyone, this took me a long time to write!

FLOYD 2. I want my money!

MR. TRUNDLE 1. *(Trying to stay in control.)* Let me explain something...

MRS. STEPP 2. I want better grammar!

MR. TRUNDLE 1. We need to get this play rehearsed and on stage in exactly... *(Looking at his watch.)*

HANS 2. I want to dance!

MR. TRUNDLE 1. Thirty-six hours and two minutes!

MS. PARKER 2. Meow, meow, meow! *["I want to live!"]*

MR. TRUNDLE 1. Not helping.

MARGIE 2. I want to play a raccoon!

> *(Trying to contain himself, **MR. TRUNDLE** grabs **MARGIE** by the shoulders and sits her down.)*

MR. TRUNDLE 1. Or something terrible is going to happen!
*(To **FLOYD**.)* Your lumberyard will be gone,
*(To **MRS. STEPP**.)* your school will be gone,
*(To **MS. PARKER**.)* your library will be gone, and all your homes, everything you have worked for your entire lives, will become worthless. And where is Joe?! Can anyone tell me where Joe is?!

MS. PARKER 2. Mr. Trundle, why don't you and I step outside for a moment?

(She guides **MR. TRUNDLE** *out of the room. They circle the stage and are now outside.)*

MR. TRUNDLE 1. I'm sorry, Ms. Parker, I can't. I tried jumping in the deep end. Clearly, I'm not the man for this job.

(**MS. PARKER** *takes him by the arm and walks him down the street.)*

MS. PARKER 2. Nonsense. Mr. Trundle, Popcorn Falls attracts a very particular type of person.

MR. TRUNDLE 1. Unhinged?

MS. PARKER 2. Scared. People who feel their dreams are without merit. Unimportant. No larger than a kernel of popcorn itself. When I arrived here, many years ago, I had dreams of opening a book store. Used books, new books, rare books. Floyd wanted to make art sculptures and fine furniture. Mrs. Stepp wanted to open a dress shop, design clothing.

Suddenly those dreams are within reach. You've presented us with hope, Mr. Trundle. And hope can scare the living daylights out of you.

MR. TRUNDLE 1. Yeah, well, let's hope I can figure out how to write a play. Fast.

MS. PARKER 2. Dig deep. Find your strength. Start your theater and save Popcorn Falls! If not for us, for yourself.

MR. TRUNDLE 1. You're good. You know that?

(**MR. TRUNDLE** *writes "27 Delaware Lane" on the board.)*

MS. PARKER 2. I have always depended on the kindness of strangers.

MR. TRUNDLE 1. I read that one. She ends up in the loony bin.

[MUSIC NO. 15]

MS. PARKER 2. Good night, sweet prince. Parting is such sweet sorrow, that I shall say good night 'til we rehearse tomorrow.

(She disappears behind the chalkboard.)

Scene Twelve: Joe's House

(**MR. TRUNDLE** *approaches Joe's front porch, overhearing* **JOE** *talking to his four boys.*)

JOE 2. *(Offstage.)* Okay, boys, lunch is over. Let's all put our shoes on and get ready to go.

(**MR. TRUNDLE** *knocks.*)

(Offstage.) Oh, Christ.

(**JOE** *enters.*)

MR. TRUNDLE 1. Hey. We missed you at rehearsals, Joe.

JOE 2. Yeah...this isn't a good time.

MR. TRUNDLE 1. Look, I don't know what's going on but we're running out of time.

JOE 2. I have to get Trudy to her check-up and the babysitter canceled so I got to get four boys fed, dressed and out the door in three minutes.

(Calling offstage.) You heard what I said, put your shoes on!

(To **MR. TRUNDLE**.*)* That's what's going on.

MR. TRUNDLE 1. I thought we were a team. I can't do this by myself.

JOE 2. Why don't you get Becky to help?

MR. TRUNDLE 1. Can we leave Becky out of this? Look, we still have a day and a half. I made a new schedule. We start tomorrow morning.

(*He hands* **JOE** *the script, then turns to go.*)

JOE 2. And what do you suggest I do with the kids?

MR. TRUNDLE 1. I don't know. Bring them to rehearsal. That way you don't need a babysitter.

JOE 2. Perfect! Sure. I'll bring them to the lumberyard. I'll set one pair on the table saw while the other two play with a nail gun.

(*He pushes the script back into* **MR. TRUNDLE***'s hands.*)

MR. TRUNDLE 1. We can't let them win, Joe.

JOE 2. I'm not looking to win. I'm looking to get through the day.

MR. TRUNDLE 1. We need to put on a play!

JOE 2. Your play is bad, Mr. Trundle!

MR. TRUNDLE 1. Which is it, Joe? What's the excuse today? First it was Becky, then it's the kids, now it's my bad play?

> (**JOE** *turns to go.*)

You chickened out, Joe. That's why it upset you to see Becky. "What could have been" has come back to look you square in the eye and you don't like it.

JOE 2. What do you know about it?

MR. TRUNDLE 1. I know plenty. This isn't about Becky. This is about you! You're scared and full of regrets and looking for someone to blame. Well, join the club! And, by the way, if you loved her, you would have left with her.

> (**JOE** *punches* **MR. TRUNDLE.** *They both are in shock.* **JOE** *waits for a moment, then heads to the door.*)

JOE 2. *(To his kids.)* It's okay, buddy. Daddy's fine. Tell Mommy we're ready to go.

> (*He looks to* **MR. TRUNDLE,** *then goes into the house.*)

[MUSIC NO. 16]

Scene Thirteen: Mr. Doyle's Office

> (**ACTOR 2** *plays both* **MR. DOYLE** *and* **AUSTIN**
> *by way of the cunning use of a baseball cap*
> *and a pair of glasses.* **ACTOR 1** *becomes* **MISS**
> **BROWN** *– a very unenthusiastic secretary*
> *who is focused on polishing her nails.*)

MISS BROWN 1. *(Pressing buzzer on desk.)* Beep. Mr. Doyle, your three o'clock is here.

MR. DOYLE 2. *(Pressing the buzzer on his desk.)* Beep. Thank you, Miss Brown. Send the boy in.

AUSTIN 2. You called me, sir?

MR. DOYLE 2. Let me get straight to the point. It's fallen on my shoulders to make a decision that could affect the future of Popcorn Falls forever...who will be the next chief of police?

AUSTIN 2. That is amazing sir, that is exactly what I wanted to talk to you about!

MISS BROWN 1. Beep! Mr. Doyle, don't forget your mani/pedi in thirty minutes.

MR. DOYLE 2. Beep! Goodie.

(Back to Austin.) I need to find someone who isn't afraid to take responsibility. Someone strong enough to be head of security while my plant is being built. Someone who knows this town like the back of their hand!

AUSTIN 2. *(Jumping up and down.)* Me! Me! Pick me!

MISS BROWN 1. Beep! Mr. Doyle, your wife called. You need to pick up Mr. Doyle Jr. from Pee-Wee Karate.

MR. DOYLE 2. Beep! *(With a deep bow.)* Arigato gozaimasu. *[Thank you.]*

(Back to Austin.) I have a plan and I need someone to help me. We're going to give the people of Popcorn exactly what they want – water. And then I'm going to give you what you want. One day, all of this will be yours...Police Chief Austin.

AUSTIN 2. *(Doing a bell kick.)* Hot Diggity Dog!

> (**MR. DOYLE** *puts his arm around Austin, whispering in his ear [the side of the hat] as he walks him offstage.*)

MR. DOYLE 2. Now, here's my plan. First...

> *(Incomprehensible mumble.)*

...and then...

> *(Continues with incomprehensible mumbling as they exit.)*

[MUSIC NO. 17]

Scene Fourteen - The Falls

(MR. TRUNDLE writes "The Falls" on the board, then leans on the back of a chair. Maybe he picks up a rock and throws it. BECKY approaches.)

BECKY 2. *(Making light.)* Your burger's getting cold.

(MR. TRUNDLE acknowledges her.)

I used to play here at the falls when I was a kid. I kept waiting for George Washington to return. I didn't really care about him but I'd never seen a horse up close and I thought that would be pretty neat. I didn't realize he'd been dead for two hundred years.

MR. TRUNDLE 1. I'm so tired. I just want to sleep.

BECKY 2. "To sleep, perchance to dream." You're a strong man, Mr. Trundle.

MR. TRUNDLE 1. I'm a fraud. To be honest. A guy who thought he could hide out in a quiet little town and pull his life back together. A guy who can't figure out how to end a story. Who isn't even sure how to begin one.

(He turns enough so BECKY can see his face.)

BECKY 2. What happened to your lip?

MR. TRUNDLE 1. I ran headlong into a fist.

(Preempting her question.) I deserved it, believe me. I used to think I was only mean when I drank. Mistake number four thousand, three hundred and twenty-eight.

BECKY 2. Mr. Trundle, coming back home was probably the hardest thing I've ever done. I never became an actress. I met a guy, it lasted six months, and now I have a daughter who sleeps in a sewing room. Do you know how many times I wanted to give up and throw myself into the falls? Well, back when we had falls. You'll see. Someday you'll look back and...you'll see that everything worked out just as it was supposed to. And all that...all those mistakes...they brought you here.

MR. TRUNDLE 1. You're young.

BECKY 2. There's nothing I can do about that. I have to pick up Lydia from Pee-Wee Karate.

> *(Beat.)*

I know what mean looks like, Mr. Trundle. That's not you.

> *(She turns to go.)*

Looks like rain.

> *(She erases "The Falls," then exits.)*

[MUSIC NO. 18]

> *(**MR. TRUNDLE** grabs his script and exits, then enters from another door carrying a suitcase. He crosses the stage.)*

> *(**JOE** runs on. Clearly he has been looking for **MR. TRUNDLE**. The men meet center. Things are tense and awkward.)*

Scene Fifteen: Bus Stop

JOE 2. Hey.

MR. TRUNDLE 1. Hey.

JOE 2. You're a hard man to find.

MR. TRUNDLE 1. Yeah, well...

JOE 2. Look... I'm sorry.

MR. TRUNDLE 1. No, let's not...

JOE 2. The pressure got to me...

MR. TRUNDLE 1. It was my fault.

JOE 2. I lost my head.

MR. TRUNDLE 1. I pushed you. I shouldn't have said those things.

JOE 2. No, what you said was right. All of it.

(He pulls a sonogram from his pocket.)

But look... I'm going to have a daughter. Trudy's check-up. Look at the sonogram. One of the twins is a girl. Five sons but I'll finally have a girl. And she's going to grow up. And if we don't do this play, if we don't save this town...how do I look her in the face?

(Noticing the suitcase.)

What's with the suitcase?

MR. TRUNDLE 1. I screwed up, Joe.

(He writes "Bus Stop" on the board.)

Everything in my life. Everything I have touched. I can blame it on my drinking, I can blame it on Marilyn, I can blame it on Jeffrey Cooper. But the truth is...if I stay here I'll only screw up someone else.

(He turns to go. **JOE** *blocks him.)*

JOE 2. You can't leave, Mr. Trundle.

MR. TRUNDLE 1. *(Hands him script.)* You want to put on a play, have at it. I need to catch my bus.

(He crosses the stage. **JOE** *follows.)*

JOE 2. Independence! No more being dependent on the tyrant. That's what George Washington would say! Keep your water Cattaraugus or we shall make tea from it.

MR. TRUNDLE 1. Are you drunk?

(He sits at the "bus stop," his suitcase next to him.)

JOE 2. People will eat before they go to the theater. They'll drink in our bars. Shop in our stores.

MR. TRUNDLE 1. Will you wake the hell up?! We don't have a theater. We have a librarian who thinks she's a cat, an oversexed sixth grade teacher who would make a pass at a kumquat, and a one-armed lumberyard owner who really, really gives me the creeps. We have a town of losers who will one day work in a sewage factory. Someday your daughter will be able to say, "My dad can turn manure into drinking water." And to top it all off, my play stinks!

JOE 2. You'll fix it.

MR. TRUNDLE 1. I don't know how! It's a stupid play about cats and trees and a hopeless love story. It's nothing like the plays we read.

JOE 2. What about Becky?! You were right... I don't want Becky. But you do. You're just going to walk away from that?

*(Places script on **MR. TRUNDLE**'s lap.)*

For Becky. For my daughter.

*(**MR. TRUNDLE** looks at the script...then drops it to the floor.)*

Fine. You want to go? Run. If I had half a brain, I'd leave with you. A town of losers. That's what we got. Losers who thought they could do the impossible. That would be something to see. "The theater that tried to save Popcorn Falls." What a farce!

*(He just gave **MR. TRUNDLE** an idea.)*

MR. TRUNDLE 1. That's it...

JOE 2. So, fine...you want to leave? Go!

> (**MR. TRUNDLE** *grabs the script and starts writing.*)

MR. TRUNDLE 1. That's it!

JOE 2. What are you doing?

MR. TRUNDLE 1. Joe, go to Suzy's! Get us some coffee...get us an entire pot of coffee!

JOE 2. What are you talking about?

MR. TRUNDLE 1. Joe, I'm going to write a play. A real play. With a part for everyone in this town.

JOE 2. But how are we going to...

MR. TRUNDLE 1. Tomorrow morning. Ten a.m. Call Ms. Parker. Call Floyd. Call everyone!

JOE 2. I'm calling Becky. *(He turns to go.)*

MR. TRUNDLE 1. No. I already tried, Joe.

JOE 2. We're putting on a play. Becky's the only one who knows how!

MR. TRUNDLE 1. But...

JOE 2. I know Becky, Mr. Trundle. She'll do it. Trust me.

MR. TRUNDLE 1. We're going to put on a play.

> (**JOE** *runs off.*)

Joe, we are going to put on a play!!

[MUSIC NO. 19]

Scene Sixteen: Lumberyard

(This is the rehearsal of the play Mr. Trundle and Joe wrote. **BECKY** *sits at the table making the sound of a sewing machine. She "sews" the apron shirt while looking at script pages.* **HANS** *enters with a "Ding-a-ling." He also holds pages. He is a bit awkward.)*

HANS 1. Becky! You're vorking in Mrs. Stepp's dress shop now?

BECKY 2. Beats slinging burgers and pulling beers. Plus it gives me nights off for my acting classes over in Peepaw.

HANS 1. *(Looking around.)* Vow, business is really booming, ja?! Do you make suits? I need to place an order for Mr. Upmall.

BECKY 2. Oh, no, did he...the poor dear.

HANS 1. Poor, nussing! He's getting married at ninety-three. Ven Ms. Parker proposed, he keeled right over...

HANS 1 & BECKY 2. ...Just like one of those YouTube goats!

BECKY 2. Let's talk pattern.

(She walks to the American flag, draping it over her arm.)

How about something...patriotic?

HANS 1. Ooh, goose steps!

BECKY 2. Goosebumps?

HANS 1. Zat's the vun.

BECKY 2. I'll get started on this right away.

HANS 1. Give my best to Ted.

(He exits with a "Ding-a-ling." **BECKY** *steps forward, looking out the window.)*

BECKY 2. Huh...looks like rain. Or maybe not.

*(**MR. TRUNDLE** runs onstage.)*

MR. TRUNDLE 1. Aaand blackout! "The End!"

MS. PARKER 2. Callooh Callay! A happy ending!

MR. TRUNDLE 1. Great rehearsal everyone! With seventy-eight minutes to spare!

> (**MS. PARKER** *takes a deep bow as* **MR. TRUNDLE** *continues.*)

Let's get everything loaded on the truck and get it to the town hall as quickly as possible!

> (*He turns to leave, but* **BECKY** *grabs his arm, swinging him around.*)

BECKY 2. You really are lovely with words.

MR. TRUNDLE 1. We better get to the theater.

BECKY 2. Right.

> (*They cross each other –* **HANS** *and* **MR. TRUNDLE** *jump out from each side of* **BECKY**.)

HANS 1. Hold it! No vun's goin' novere! Ve've been ka-shtinkled! Ze truck has a flat tire!

MR. TRUNDLE 1. What?!

HANS 1. I zuzpect foul play.

MR. TRUNDLE 1. You think we were sabotaged?

MARGIE 2. I know how to fix a flat.

MR. TRUNDLE 1. You do?

MARGIE 2. Obviously!

MR. TRUNDLE 1. Thank you, Margie! Just hurry. We have to put on the play by eight o'clock. On the dot. I mean it! Not one minute late!

BECKY 2. (*On phone.*) What? Mom, slow down...the bridge is...oh, no!

> (*To* **MR. TRUNDLE**.) They've blockaded the bridge.

MR. TRUNDLE 1. What?

BECKY 2. The police won't let anyone through. We can't get to the theater! Look!

MR. TRUNDLE 1. (*Crossing* **BECKY**.) What are we going to do?

JOE 2. The riverbed! We can drive across the dry riverbed.

MR. TRUNDLE 1. How?

JOE 2. There's a low spot behind Suzy's.

MR. TRUNDLE 1. Then what are we waiting for?! Everyone to their stations!!

BECKY 2. I knew you could do it.

> (*She gives* **MR. TRUNDLE** *a kiss on the cheek.*)

MR. TRUNDLE 1. Oh. Wow.

> (*He starts off.*)

BECKY 2. Ted!

MR. TRUNDLE 1. I know what you're going to say and I feel the same way. I think I felt it the first time we spoke. And I didn't know if you felt the same way, and I have Marilyn and you have Lydia, who thinks we could make something beautiful together in bed, and I love children! I just want you to know that...with all my heart! I've always wanted to have children!

BECKY 2. I was going to say... (*Picking up suitcase.*) ...would you mind taking the suitcase full of props?

MR. TRUNDLE 1. Yes. Props. I will take the...
(*Grabbing suitcase.*) Ohmygod, ohmygod, ohmygod...

> (*As he crosses* **BECKY** *she spins him around, kissing him. They pull away.*)

I'm *[actor's age]*.

BECKY 2. I'm twenty-seven.

> (*Together, they put the suitcase down.*)

BECKY 2 & MR. TRUNDLE 1. I don't care!

> (*They kiss again, longer.*)

MR. TRUNDLE 1. I really do love kids.

BECKY 2. Note taken! Now, GO!!

> (**MR. TRUNDLE** *releases the retractable suitcase handle.*)

MR. TRUNDLE 1. I'll run ahead. Tell Margie...

> (*He straddles the suitcase.*)

I took her bike.

(Rings bell.) "Ring-ring." "Once more, dear kernels, unto the breach!"

> *(He "rides" the suitcase off like it's a bike.)*
> **[MUSIC NO. 20]**

Scene Seventeen: Mr. Doyle's Office

> (**ACTOR 2** *draws a large water spigot on the board, then becomes* **MR. DOYLE** *looking through binoculars [two empty soda cans from the garbage].* **MR. TRUNDLE** *puts on the* **AUSTIN** *hat and grabs the blue umbrella. He becomes* **AUSTIN,** *facing upstage, standing at the Popcorn Falls Dam release valve [the blue umbrella].* **ACTOR 2** *does both voices as* **AUSTIN** *pantomimes talking into his walkie-talkie [eraser].*)

MR. DOYLE 2. Drive across the dry riverbed, will they?

AUSTIN 2. Ready at the dam, sir!

MR. DOYLE 2. Patience, dear boy. We don't want to spoil our little surprise. The truck! The truck is approaching! Be ready!

AUSTIN 2. Ready?

MR. DOYLE 2. Ready!

AUSTIN 2. Which way do I turn it?

MR. DOYLE 2. To the left, you idiot, I told you, to the left!

AUSTIN 2. Left?!

MR. DOYLE 2. Left!

AUSTIN 2. Now?!

MR. DOYLE 2. Now!

ACTORS 1 & 2. NOOOOOWWWW!!!!

> (*Music out.* **AUSTIN** *turns the release valve [umbrella]. He then uses the twirling blue umbrella to indicate water filling the stage as he makes the sound effects of gushing water.*)

MR. DOYLE 2. Goodbye, Popcorn Community Players! Hope you all know how to swim!

> (**ACTOR 1** *twirls the umbrella in front of* **ACTOR 2**'s *face, placing the* **AUSTIN** *cap on* **ACTOR 2**'s *head, then moves away, still twirling the umbrella.*)

AUSTIN 2. *(Into walkie-talkie.)* Mr. Doyle! There's a bunch of state troopers waving their arms at me! Hey fellas! *(Getting scared.)* What? What?
(Slowly raises his hands in the air.) No! No, it wasn't me. It wasn't me!

> *(Again,* **ACTOR 1** *twirls the umbrella in front of* **ACTOR 2***'s face and removes the hat.* **MR. DOYLE** *is again holding cans as binoculars.)*

MR. DOYLE 2. So long, Austin! See you in ten to twenty!

> *(***ACTOR 1** *twirls the umbrella in front of* **MR. DOYLE***'s face, handing it to him.)*

Scene Eighteen: Town Hall

(**MR. TRUNDLE** *mimes phone.*)

MR. TRUNDLE 1. Becky? Becky, where are you?

(**ACTOR 2** *crosses back and forth onstage, twirling the umbrella. He becomes all the characters bobbing up and down behind the umbrella, "floating down the river." He pops up for each character.*)

BECKY 2. We're in the set!

MR. TRUNDLE 1. Where?

BECKY 2. We're in the set! Floating down the river!

MS. PARKER 2. Weeee! It's like the log ride at Wally World!

BECKY 2. Someone turned on the water just as the truck was crossing. Most of us were in the back holding down the set and now we're floating in it.

MRS. STEPP 2. My body hasn't moved up and down like this in years!

FLOYD 2. I'll bet you're glad now I added that insulation!

MRS. STEPP 2. Oh Floyd, when are we going to stop?! I love you, Floyd.

FLOYD 2. Look at me. I'll never be able to hold you in my arms.

MRS. STEPP 2. As long as I have your heart, I don't care what other pieces are missing!

BECKY 2. Joe, what are you doing?!

MR. TRUNDLE 1. Becky, what's going on?!

BECKY 2. Joe just dove into the water!

MR. TRUNDLE 1. What?!

BECKY 2. He's using the ASPCA sign as a boogie board!

MR. TRUNDLE 1. Where are you?!

BECKY 2. *(Trying to read street sign.)* We're crossing... Delaware! We'll get on dry land once we get to the spill-off in Munsy. But we'll never get to the theater in time. *(Breaking up.)* I...sorry...love...

(She goes down behind the umbrella.)

MR. TRUNDLE 1. Becky, you're breaking up! Becky, I can't hear you! Hello?! Hello?!!

> *(**MR. DOYLE** pops up from behind the umbrella, dropping it over his shoulder.)*

MR. DOYLE 2. Hello.

MR. TRUNDLE 1. Doyle!

MR. DOYLE 2. Your Island of Misfit Toys is sinking, Mr. Trundle.

MR. TRUNDLE 1. I knew this was you!

MR. DOYLE 2. Hope. Remember that, Mr. Trundle. Before you drop someone in the middle of the ocean be sure they're tethered to your finger by a small thread of hope. Give them something to swim toward...a distant buoy...and as their arms weaken...as they struggle for air...they'll never feel the wallet being pulled from their pocket.

MR. TRUNDLE 1. You're a snake, you know that? A worm!

MR. DOYLE 2. Your harsh words cut me as would a grapefruit spoon.

(Pointing offstage.) And look! The day is saved. Here comes your plumber!

> *(He points to the back of the house, then turns into **JOE** running up the aisle.)*

MR. TRUNDLE 1. My plumber?!

JOE 2. *(Can be pre-recorded.)* Executive custodian!

MR. TRUNDLE 1. Joe! How did you get here so fast?!

JOE 2. On a tidal wave of independence! We have water, Mr. Trundle! The falls are flowing!

MR. TRUNDLE 1. You hear that, Mr. Doyle? This time, you're not going to win!

MR. DOYLE 2. Oh, yes I will. I've just flushed your little troupe of miscreants down the sewer. Had you written a show with only two people, you would have been fine. But you had to be the savior to all. Well, look where it's got you! As the water is flowing from the north, I assume you'll be leaving to the south. We'll be waiting.

> *(He exits with his usual cackle.* **MR. TRUNDLE** *goes to yell after him.)*

MR. TRUNDLE 1. You better sleep with one eye open, Doyle, because one day we dreamers will realize there are a lot more of us than there are of you, and we will huff and puff and blow down your damned dam and wipe out everything you stand for! You cackling sunuva bitch.

> *(***JOE** *runs on.)*

JOE 2. Mr. Trundle, it's 7:58! Only two minutes left!

MR. TRUNDLE 1. Ugh...think! Come on, Mr. Pickles! You're the one with the bright ideas. Think!

> *(***JOE** *grabs the two erasers. Banging them together, he creates a cloud of chalk that he steps into to create* **MS. PARKER** *as a memory.)*

MS. PARKER 2. Dig deep. Find your strength! Start your theater and save Popcorn Falls! If not for us, for yourself... *(Claps erasers.)* ...yourself... *(Claps erasers.)* ...your–

MR. TRUNDLE 1. Wait a minute.

MS. PARKER 2. *(Claps erasers.)* – Self.

MR. TRUNDLE 1. I think I'm getting an idea.

> *(***MS. PARKER** *bangs the erasers together again; stepping into the cloud of chalk, she becomes* **MR. DOYLE** *as a memory.)*

MR. DOYLE 2. Had you written a show with only two people, you would have been fine... *(Claps erasers.)* ...two people you would have been fine... *(Claps erasers.)*

MR. DOYLE 2 & MR. TRUNDLE 1. ...Two people...

MR. DOYLE 2. ...You would have been fine...

MR. TRUNDLE 1. Yes! Joe! Get ready to put on a play.

> *(He sets the stage for the top of the show.)*

JOE 2. WHAT?! What are you talking about? We don't have costumes!

MR. TRUNDLE 1. Don't need them.

JOE 2. We don't have sets!

MR. TRUNDLE 1. A compelling story, that's what makes a good play!

JOE 2. We don't have any actors.

MR. TRUNDLE 1. Sure we do.

JOE 2. Who, you and me?!

MR. TRUNDLE 1. You were "class clown," remember?!

JOE 2. That's because I was always stoned.

MR. TRUNDLE 1. And I'm a politician! If I know how to do anything – it's act!

JOE 2. *(Getting on board.)* "A happy ending, the good guys get what they want!"

MR. TRUNDLE 1. And I want Becky. I've wanted her from the moment you kissed me!

JOE 2. And I want Trudy. And my four kids. And my two unpopped kernels.

MR. TRUNDLE 1. We're gonna make your kids proud! We'll do *The Sound of Music* and put 'em all on stage! Yes – musicals! We'll have two theaters. One for the big shows and one for the small shows. The kind with the small casts!

JOE 2. *(Turning front.)* Mrs. Stepp's Dress Shop! We'll put that next to the theater.

MR. TRUNDLE 1. And Floyd's Furniture! And next to that, Ms. Parker's Used Books!

(Referring to the banner overhead.) And this is what our play is about...Popcorn Falls!

JOE 2. No! From now on...Popcorn Rises!

　　　　(They hug.)

I was going to tell you this later...I'm naming my son after you.

MR. TRUNDLE 1. Thank you.

JOE 2. I'll have my very own...Mr. Trundle.

(They hug again. **MR. TRUNDLE** *looks at his watch.)*

MR. TRUNDLE 1. Are you ready?

(They slowly turn out to look at the audience.)

JOE 2. Dear God, I hope so.

[MUSIC NO. 21]

(The over-dramatic music kicks into high gear. They run around stage mirroring what they did at the top of the show. **MR. TRUNDLE** *proudly carries the mic stand across the stage, and when it hits the ground...)*

(Music out.)

MR. TRUNDLE 1. *(Rehearsing, in a calm, flat tone.)* Good evening, ladies and gentlemen. As the new mayor of Popcorn Falls, it gives me great pleasure to introduce the chief executive officer of Cattaraugus County, Mr. Doyle. How about a big Popcorn...how about a big... how about a big...
(Tapping on the mic.) Hello? Hello?
(Shouting to the back of the room.) Joe? Hey, Joe?! Can you hear me?!

(He looks front with a huge smile.)

JOE 2. *(Offstage.)* Loud and clear, Mr. Trundle! Loud and clear!

(Blackout.)

[Option: the lights can also blackout after "Good evening, ladies and gentlemen." In this case, **MR. TRUNDLE** *would do the line with a big smile as the lights blackout.)*

[MUSIC NO. 22]

(Curtain Call – One by one they circle the chalkboard, coming out to bow as each character. Some characters will have to

double up – **MRS. STEPP** *and* **FLOYD** *can bow together, as can* **BECKY** *and* **LYDIA**. *Finally,* **ACTORS 1** *and* **2** *come out. They bow together.)*

[MUSIC NO. 23]

End of Play

PROPS

Small Mesh Garbage Can – So the audience can see its contents:

> Empty liquor bottle
>
> Blue umbrella
>
> A few crumpled pieces of paper
>
> Two soda cans (these will become binoculars)

Austin's hat – baseball hat that becomes Austin's police hat

Doyle's glasses – thick, dark glasses

Striped sweater – will become "Mr. Cuddles," Ms. Parker's cat

Gingham shirt – will become Becky's apron and Lydia's dress

Two blank writing pads

Blank piece of paper in white envelope – Doyle's contract

Hans' monocle

Cell phone – Joe will carry this phone. He will use it as Joe, Margie, and Becky.

Joe's rag – To be carried in Joe's back pocket. Becomes Mrs. Omki's babushka and Becky's bar rag.

Pastor Pete's priest collar and glasses – The collar should have elastic on the back so it can go on and off very quickly.

Small flower in vase that falls apart when placed on table – This was accomplished by placing magnets at the base of the flower.

Handful of hardcover books – plays

Baby powder – to put in two of the erasers to create dust

Carry-on-sized suitcase on rollers with retractable arm

SET PIECES

Mic in stand

Mic cord, frayed at end

2 light chairs that can be moved around quickly

1 café-sized table

1 small bookshelf about waist-high – This will become the Sudsy Mug on one side, and the "library" on the other. May want to be on wheels or gliders so it moves quickly

1 American flag on a pole

1 sturdy coatrack

1 chalkboard with chalk and four erasers – The chalkboard should be on wheels so it can move quickly.